Lock Down Publications and Ca$h
Presents

FRESH
OFF DA
PORCH 2
TOO FAR GONE

Written By
IRA B.

Lock Down Publications
P.O. Box 944
Stockbridge, GA 30281
www.lockdownpublications.com

Like our page on Facebook: Lock Down Publications
www.facebook.com/lockdownpublications.ldp

Stay Connected with Us!

Text **LOCKDOWN** to 22828 to stay up-to-date with new releases, sneak peaks, contests and more…

Like our page on Facebook:
Lock Down Publications

Join Lock Down Publications/The New Era Reading Group

Visit our website:
www.lockdownpublications.com

Follow us on Instagram:
Lock Down Publications

Email Us: We want to hear from you!

Dedication

I dedicate this book to Anthony "Buckey" Fields, bestselling author of the *Ultimate Sacrifice* series. You are the real one, big bro. I salute you. Your contribution to the readers is very appreciated.

Chapter 1

"Don't let me die, cuz!" screamed Rontay in the backseat, as he bled profusely. Lank was pressing against the stomach wound as hard as he could to stop or slow down the flow of blood coming from the gunshot hole.

Rontay was also coughing up blood, and Lank could hear the telltale sign of death approaching.

"Hurry the fuck up, Lil E!" Lank desperately replied.

Lil Earl said, "I'm pushin' this bitch, brah!"

"Please, Earl, hurry up. My cousin is dying!"

"We almost there, my nigga." Lil Earl could see the hospital coming up, as he floored the car past one hundred twenty miles per hour to get there.

Rontay stared up at his cousin. "Tell Mama… I love… her, cuz!" He coughed some more, as Lank felt a sprinkle of blood and mucus shoot up to his face.

"Don't talk like that, Rontay. You gon' live to tell her ya'self," replied Lank. He was surprised to hear his cousin say those words regarding his mother. For a very long time, Rontay had grown to hate his mother, Glenda Long, who was a well-known crackhead. She had brought him so much pain and humiliation throughout the years that Rontay had once considered killing her. Once, she had tried to use him as collateral to purchase drugs from her dealer. Rontay was just at the tender age of ten years old when that happened. It was right then that he was convinced that his mother really didn't love him.

Not even a little bit.

She was selfish.

But now here Rontay was, declaring his love for the woman who had caused his life to be a living hell.

"Hold on!" Lil Earl replied moments before yanking the wheel right to swing the car into the hospital's entrance. The car screeched up the pathway leading up to the main building of the ER reception entrance.

Fortunately for them, a pair of paramedics were coming out of the emergency room exit doors when the car swerved to a halt before them. Lil Earl jumped out immediately and demanded that they come do something about Rontay's situation.

Rontay was promptly taken into the ER and then immediately into the operation room.

After seeing his cousin get carted through the doors on a gurney, Lank decided not to wait around in case the authorities came out demanding answers. So, he hurried back to the car where Lil Earl was already sliding back behind the wheel.

And that was when he saw her. Brandi. She had come rushing out the door from the ER exit. Then, Lank felt everything in him awaken at the sight of her.

"Larry?" she called out to him.

Lank stared at her longingly, unsure of how he should react to this. Brandi was his girl, but they had issues, and those issues had hindered their relationship. It had been a week or so since they'd seen each other.

"What happened to Rontay?" She hurried over to him.

"This ain't the time, Brandi," he said.

She gave him a strange look. "You okay? I'm worried about you, Larry."

"I'm good," he answered.

"No, you're not," she said. "Look at yourself." Brandi gestured toward his bloody clothes, and he stared down at himself in silence with a forlorn look.

"Brah!?" Lil Earl shouted impatiently.

Glancing back at his road dawg, Lank turned back to Brandi and said, "I miss you, B-Love."

"I miss you too," she said in what sounded like a whine. "Larry, we need to talk, like seriously."

"Later." Lank turned toward the car.

"But what if later never comes?"

Hearing the fear in her voice made him stop short, then he turned around and hurried back over to her. When he did this, Brandi instinctively pulled him into an awkward embrace. His bloody clothes weren't important to her, just the assurance of their love and having each other close again.

"I promise I'll come back for you."

"But you've said that too many times before." Brandi shivered in his arms with her face pressed into his hard chest. "I want it to be real this time."

"I mean it this time," he vowed.

"You said that before too."

"Lank!" Lil Earl was losing his patience.

Lank kissed her on the forehead. Then, he pulled away from her embrace. "I gotta go, B-Love."

"Be careful," she told him.

He kissed her again and ran for the car and jumped into the passenger seat. "Let's ride, my nigga!"

All you heard was car tires squealing, as Lil Earl sent the engine roaring toward the main highway.

Back in traffic, Lank put a call in to his Aunt Faye to go be with Rontay. This was Jay Baby's mother, Rontay's mother's baby sister, and the first cousin of Jerome Turner, who was Amanda's father. After hanging up with his auntie, Lank finally came to the conclusion on what he needed to do.

"I gotta hit them niggas back now," said Lank. "It's only right that I do, brah."

"Like I don' told you already before, my nigga, I'm down for whateva'," said Lil Earl. In his heart of hearts, he was really feeling some type of way about Bizkit being killed the way he was. Bizkit was his friend, his brotha; however, Lil Earl was just buying time until he had the perfect opportunity to actually avenge his death.

"Yeah. That shit hurt my family. I gotta clap back."

"Who first?" asked Lil Earl.

"Who else?" Lank gave him a serious look. "Right now, Twan is more of a threat than the others. He's their leader, so it'll be best to knock his block off *off top*."

"Twan ain't the only one a serious threat tho."

"All them niggas is, brah. But if we can catch them all together, then we punish them niggas. I won't be able to sleep at night knowin' I let them niggas hurt my family and didn't do nothin' about it." Lank thought back on his Aunt Faye's cries when he told her about Rontay and Jay Baby. She pretty much blamed him for what happened, and it hurt to hear her say that shit.

"I know a way we can hit them easily."

Lank gazed over at him. "All Twan had left was his sista, Alisha, brah. So, we can't use her. Then, the lil' nigga, Cody, it's gon' be hard trappin' him wit'out involvin' other muthafuckas who'll fuck up the mission. Because everybody he love and care about is at the hospital right now and gettin' to them to trap him…"

"I was thinkin' about Shana," said Lil Earl.

Silence.

"Use Shana to bring Money Mel to us, and nine times outta ten, the rest of them gon' follow," Lil Earl added, as he drove past the county courthouse downtown. He made sure that he drove the speed limit so as to not cause them any reason to get pulled over.

No response from Lank.

Is this nigga crazy? thought Lank. *He wants to use Brandi's sister as bait?* He knew how that would affect their relationship because then Lil Earl would have to kill Shana too. And what if something went wrong, and Brandi found

8

out that he was involved? That would open up a whole other can of worms that he could live without.

"Lemme guess," said Lil Earl. "You don't wanna put Shana through all that?"

"Because it'll involve B-Love," he replied.

"But what's more important, Lank? Your bitch's broken heart or your loyalty to your family?"

"Don't do that, brah."

"I'm just keepin' it one hunnid wit' you, my nigga. Because at this stage, you gotta put your pride to the side and make your heart turn cold," Lil Earl stressed. "Retaliation is a must."

Lank didn't say anything.

How could he deny the truth?

***

At first, Daisy didn't know how close to home this whole situation had brought her. Before coming to Quincy, she was only thinking about Avery and how they were going to go about finding him and killing him. Then, she got the disturbing confirmation from a Facebook link in regard to their current predicament.

The link had come from her cousin, Rikah, after she saw the video Mane showed them earlier and inquired about Cody. The second she saw him, she knew he looked familiar, but Daisy hadn't seen her little cousin in so damn long. It had been damn near eight years since she'd last seen Cody, but she couldn't say the same about Tami. Tami worked at a high rating hair salon in Tallahassee, and Daisy frequently saw her in the big city hanging out with friends.

Rikah, whose mother, Sheryl, was Tami's aunt, had been very vivid in her text regarding the situation they were faced with. She said for Daisy to find out what she could and report back to her. Rikah was boss status, the wifey of a thoroughbred gangster and a renowned drug lord who Daisy was grateful toward after she connected her with Von. Yeah, it was due to Rikah's influence that Daisy and Von were one another's most trusted comrades.

It was Rikah who was the big dawg.

Von was more the chief's enforcer that made sure everything ran smoothly.

What a major coincidence it was that they had come to seek revenge against the best friend of Daisy's little cousin, Cody.

That was why Daisy made it clear to Von and Remmy that it was best that she went into the hospital alone because she wanted some personal time with Tami to learn what she needed to know to move forward. The last thing she needed was for Von to know this fact and begin to question her loyalty.

Daisy's deceased father was Tami's mother's big brother, which made them close cousins. But Daisy had long ago escaped the clutches of Quincy for the big city of Tallahassee. She was following behind Rikah who, in turn, took her in and taught her everything she knew. While Von and Remmy were invading Avery's home, Daisy took that time out to really chop it up with her cousin, Rikah, in regard to where she stood in the whole matter.

She had a serious decision to make.

"So, what's the game plan, Dee?" said Remmy after watching the whole thing transpire with the arrival of Rontay and Lank's hesitance with leaving the comfort of his woman's arms.

By this time Daisy had shared with them what she heard on her way inside the hospital, and she had explained how she manipulated her way into the loop of things concerning the nonstop bloodshed circulating throughout their small town of horrors. She told them *everything* about what was going on except for the fact that her and Tami were cousins.

"I think the best way we can…" Daisy was interrupted by a startling outburst.

"Ty! Oh, shit. That's my nigga right there!" Remmy said excitedly.

To her surprise, Daisy watched as Remmy opened the car door and got out. He called out again to the young dude who suddenly pulled up in a minivan and was dropped off outside the hospital entrance.

"Who the hell is he?" asked Daisy.

Von shrugged. "Your guess is as good as mine," she said. From her vantage point, she observed Remmy as he got the other guy's attention just before he disappeared through the entrance door. For a brief moment, Ty didn't react as he wondered who it was that called out to him. Then, once he recognized Remmy, he slowly began to navigate toward him.

"I do have a plan tho, Von," said Daisy.

"I'm listening," she sighed heavily.

Daisy said, "To get Avery, we'll have to either do one of two things: snatch his mama, Felicia, the one who we saw standin' outside smokin' earlier when that detective nigga showed up. But if we do that, we're gonna have to do it from inside or whenever she comes back out for another smoke break."

"And what's the second one?" Von watched Remmy conferring with Ty, who looked to be frustrated or something by the way he was responding.

"Or we wait till a later time after all the smoke clears and catch him slippin' then."

"I want his ass dead t'night!" snapped Von.

"But…"

"No buts, Daisy. That little muthafucker…" Von paused when the passenger door opened on her side and Remmy's frame suddenly filled the space.

"You ain't gon' believe this shit, Vee!"

"What?" She frowned at Remmy, who then pulled Ty over to take his place in front of her in the open doorway space.

"Tell her what you just told me, Ty," Remmy goaded him on with a nudge.

"He just killed my brotha and my cousin," said Ty.

"He who?" Von demanded.

Tyler McKenzie swallowed nervously. "Avery."

At hearing the name, it damn near made Von's pussy wet. Then, she scooted over across the backseat and patted the space next to her.

Remmy hurried up and jumped into the front passenger seat. He seemed so excited that he was almost giddy with what was about to transpire.

"Tell me everything," Von told Ty when he got in and closed the door. "And you better not leave nothin' out either, nigga."

And Ty did exactly what he was told.

He was from the D-Block area of Tallahassee's northside, the nephew of Tricky Nikki, a longtime trick ho who had now established herself as one of the elite members of the underworld. Remmy knew Ty due to his affiliation with the GDs, who his relatives were also affiliated with, and Remmy was well acquainted with Ty because of his reputation for madness.

Ty was a real troublemaker.

"So, you're tellin' me that Avery is still over at the house right now?" Daisy wanted to know.

He shook his head. 'Yeah. I hid in the dark not too far from the house. I watched the man take him inside, and he never came back out. I think we hurt him pretty bad tho," said Ty.

"Can you show us?" Von said.

"You know how to get back to the house, right, Ty?" asked Remmy curiously.

"I'll never forget it." Ty's voice cracked, as emotion overwhelmed him. "It's where my brotha lost his life. And my cousin," he murmured.

"And Avery's gonna pay for that," exclaimed Von.

12

"In the worst way," added Remmy.

And Detective Ray Williams too, through Von with a wicked smirk on her face.

It was time.

Chapter 2

As the words poured from Rayneshia's mouth, all Cody could do was stare at her in disbelief. Then, once the reality of her words struck dead center of his heart, Cody blacked out in a dark rage. One moment, he was standing before Rayneshia in total surprise. Then, the next moment, he had his hand gripped around her neck after forcing her back against the wall with a hard impact. Cody's menacing scowl only saw betrayal and hurt in front of him.

Rayneshia, gasping and struggling for breath, saw the murderous glare in her brother's eyes. This was that beast that they had spoken of earlier.

"Let her go, brah. That's your sista. It's not her fault." Avery had come to stand next to his brotha, facing him and seeing the viciousness in him.

Rayneshia's eyes widened with fear.

"You hear me, brah? Let her go." Avery reached up to touch Cody's arm. "Don't hurt your sista because that nigga didn't man up. Not here," he said gently, his voice low but firm. "You wouldn't do that to Ava," he said.

Cody glared at Rayneshia and roared in her face with a lion's outrage. But he let her loose, and she crumbled to the floor, crying and fighting to breathe.

That was ten minutes ago. Before Cody stormed out of the house and into the night.

At that same time, both Po'Boy and Rod, accompanied by Yak, pulled up outside the house in two separate vehicles. Rod got out and called after Cody, but Cody didn't even acknowledge him. Even Money Mel didn't know what to say when Rod looked to him for an explanation, but he didn't have any answers.

But Avery wasn't long behind his brotha, refusing to just let him out alone. Not with the endless drama that was going on around them.

When Avery caught up with him, he didn't bother saying anything, just walked alongside Cody in silence. He knew this was hard on his brotha. He knew Cody was not going to take the news lightly. So, for the next several minutes, they just trudged along in the thickness of the night's troubling atmosphere.

"She lied to me," Cody cried without shame. "That bitch lied to me all this damn time!" He slammed a fist against the palm of his hand to emphasis his point.

Avery whispered, "I know, brah."

"That bitch!" he screamed loudly.

About seventy yards back, Bebop stood at the curb outside the house, staring after them sadly.

When Cody finished releasing his frustrations into the night, Avery shared with his brotha what Rayneshia didn't get the opportunity to tell him.

While Avery talked, Cody maneuvered their destination, which happened to land them right outside his own house. He and Teddy lived the closest out of them all.

"I don't care, Av," said Cody, looking at the spot where he last saw Wesley and Corey dead right there in the front yard. You could still see the bloodstains in the grass under the moonlight.

Reaching out to tear away the yellow crime scene tape, Cody balled it up in his hand and headed straight for the front door of his house.

"You think we should go in there?" Avery didn't know the coroner had just left the scene fifteen minutes ago. They had just missed the action.

The front door was locked. Cody went around back to check the back door. Locked. "Shit."

15

"You know where to go," said Avery, referring to Cody's bedroom window that couldn't lock at all because Teddy had broken it years ago. Minutes later, after assisting his brotha up to the window, Avery was stepping through the front door. "Damn, brah." He wrinkled his nose at the smell of death thickening the air.

Quietly, Cody made his way to the kitchen where he was told Alisha had died. When he saw the bloodstains, it ached his heart. His eyes welled up in grief, but he fought back the urge. He was tired of crying. He was tired, period.

Tired of being lied to.

Tired of trusting.

He was just tired of everything and everybody.

Turning away from the kitchen doorway, Cody made his way to his bedroom. All of a sudden, he felt exhausted and quietly dropped down onto his bed.

Moments later, Avery entered the room to find Cody lying down on his back in the bed. Cody was staring up at the ceiling in silent forlorn.

"Do you hate Rayneshia?" asked Avery.

No response.

"Tell me, brah," Avery insisted.

"Why are you askin' me that shit, Av?" Cody continued to look up at the ceiling. Plastered on the ceiling of the bedroom were some posters of some of the basketball greats such as LeBron James, Vince Carter, Michael Jordan, and even Kobe Bryant. They were all Cody's idols.

"Because," said Avery, "it's not her fault, brah. I don't want you hatin' her because she had a real chance. But she ain't happy, Cody. She never was happy — she wasn't wit' that nigga!" Then, he went on to share with Cody some of Rayneshia's life failures and disappointments where their father was concerned.

"That's bullshit," said Cody. "She lived in the same house wit' tha nigga all her life."

"Okay. And?"

"He was there."

"But that doesn't mean it made her happy, brah."

No longer wanting to talk about it anymore, Cody sat up in the bed, and even that was an agonizing feat. And then, he saw something out his peripheral that made him rise up and go over to where the dresser was. Atop of the dresser was one of the five sportsmanship trophies that he'd earned over the years playing basketball and football. Beneath an MVP basketball trophy was several crinkled bills. It was the money that his mother had been caught stealing earlier — money she had not spent out of embarrassment and self-blame after she was caught red-handed. So disappointing.

"What's that for?"

Cody reminded him of what took place.

"Oh. That's it," said Avery. He knew Cody's mother could be pretty mean at times, but he would have never imagined her stealing from her own son.

That was when Cody finally glanced down at his shoes. His new pair of Air Jordans. The reason for everything. The shoes were caked with blood and dirt. Ruined. He no longer cared for the Air Jordans anymore.

"You can have mines," said Avery, seeing where Cody's mind was taking him.

"All this shit started because of these fuckin' shoes," Cody said after being snapped out of his reverie. "When Twan gave me that punk ass molly!" Angry all over again, Cody kicked the shoes off and stood there in his socked feet. Then, he saw that blood had soaked through the shoes to his socks, and that only elevated his frustration.

Avery heard his brother mumble something incoherent before he slammed open the dresser drawers and removed some clothing items. Then, without saying a word, Cody marched out of the room for the bathroom.

He left to go take a bath.

He was miserable.

A nice hot shower was just what he needed.

***

Menace panted. The heavy medication Sand had given him was wearing off. The pain was a constant burning throb. He was dizzy and scared that he might wreck the car. Menace knew it was a bad idea to be up and driving, but he was never the one to listen.

When the pain was so excruciating that it forced him out of the slumber the medication had put him in, Menace took up his phone that was found resting on the nightstand. He had a total of fourteen missed calls and eight messages. Through his pain, Menace decided to review the messages first, and that was where he got the shock of his life.

The third text message.

Alisha was dead.

Alisha. His heart, his secret love. The woman whose love for him was unfailing and always ready. Alisha had everything he had ever hoped for in a companion. What they shared together was something special. So special that Alisha wanted to run away with him so that they could live in peace.

But Twan never knew of this. He knew they cared for each other but not to that degree. Menace knew Twan would have never approved of their relationship.

Twan was overly protective about his sister.

Alisha was his world.

After allowing a few tears to escape him, Menace was then taken to that dark space where all he saw was murder and terror. That animal in him had slowly arose and taken full control of him.

Then, Lamar showed up at the height of his dark rage. Menace made that nigga lay face down on the floor and took his car keys. He wanted to shoot his bitch ass in the back of the head. But that was before he glanced up and saw little LJ peeking out through the crack of his bedroom door. So, he just took his car keys and headed out to the car and got the hell out of dodge.

Lamar was probably beating Meesha's ass right now, but that was no longer his problem.

However, the problem was him swerving down the highway, as he focused to drive straighter. Getting pulled over by the traffic patrol was not going to happen. There would be only one outcome if that ever did happen.

Another cop would die.

Or more.

So, to avoid bumping into more cops, Menace took the back roads; it was a much different route than the one he took to get there. He had a feeling the crime scene he left behind on St. John Road was still being processed and guarded. Menace knew he was a wanted man.

Menace spent the long mission back into town thinking about how he was going to approach the matter. He couldn't call because only one arm was operational. So, to get the answers he needed, he would have to take himself to where the incident took place earlier.

Back to Pepper Hill.

Soon, he was pulling the car up outside of Alisha's house at 4:21 a.m., and to his surprise, he noticed there were lights on in the house. But that wasn't the only thing he saw either. Next door at Cody's house, there were people standing out front on the porch. The porch light provided a clear view of Money Mel and two females having just approached the front door.

Then, the front door of Alisha's house opened, and there stood Rod. Menace looked at his comrade and swung the car door open immediately.

"Menace?" Rod said in surprise when Menace climbed out of the car.

And there, Menace crumbled to the ground just as he attempted to take his first step toward the truth. Blinding pain exploded through him when his body impacted with the ground. That sent Money Mel and Rod rushing to his side at once.

"My nigga, what the fuck are you doing!?" Rod scolded him, as he and Money Mel hefted him up into their arms.

"Who killed Lisha?" said Menace.

Rod didn't answer him.

"Who killed her, brah? I loved her!" Menace cried. It was all Rod needed to see to know that this was not going to be good. The declaration of Menace's true love for Alisha was about to be a serious matter to worry about. They carried Menace inside Alisha's house.

Twan was waiting.

"How I knew you was gon' pull a stunt like this?" Twan said as they deposited Menace on the sofa chair. "Your hardheaded ass just won't learn, nigga."

"Who killed Lisha?" This was all Menace wanted to know. The pain spurting through him was overshadowed by his rage, as he glared up at them.

"I knew all about you and my sista, Menace. Y'all thought you could have hidden that from me?" Twan said this in the calmest voice.

Menace watched as Twan drew his gun and stared down at him with coldness in his eyes.

"I trusted you, brah."

"So, you gon' kill me now?" said Menace.

"Kill you?" Twan looked at him in surprise, then he gazed down at the gun in his hand. "I didn't intervene because I believed in you, Menace. I trusted you to love my sista right and always protect her from harm."

"And I did, muthafucka!" he fumed.

"I know," said Twan. "That's why I'm not gonna kill you." Then, he tossed the gun to Money Mel and stepped forward to place himself in front of Menace. "You my brotha, and I love you, nigga. And I know Lisha loved you as well. She told me outta her own mouth."

"Did y'all get 'em?" Menace questioned.

Twan nodded.

"Who?"

He told Menace.

With a downcast head, Menace closed his eyes, but all he saw was Alisha's smiling face.

A lone tear fell from his eyes.

Then, his brothas hugged him. Twan cried with him, and it burned like scorching lava in their hearts.

Chapter 3

They had reached the location just as the coroner van was preparing to transport the two bodies. Trent and Draydon. From the backseat of the truck, Ty watched as the dead bodies of his eighteen-year-old brother and cousin were loaded into the back of the van.

Von gazed over at him in the dark cabin of the SUV, sensing his pain and devastation. She couldn't sympathize with him because her heart was cold.

All she knew was that something this surreal would drive a person to some very dark places.

Ty had never killed anybody a day in his life. But at that very moment, he was ready to. He wanted to kill Avery in a messy way. But he knew they wanted to kill him as well. Would that become a problem? Would Von and her crew try to cheat him out of the opportunity to murder Avery?

That wouldn't be fair and would only make him want to do something to them.

Ty wanted full revenge.

Avery was his.

Up the street ahead from where they were parked, the four of them watched the bodies being loaded into the back of the coroner's van.

A sound deep down within Ty's heart traveled up out of him when the back doors of the van shut, and it suddenly pulled away.

How was he going to explain this to his mother and his Uncle Leon? That their sons were dead and he ran away to save himself?

That was why Ty needed to do this. That was why Avery had to die tonight. Because it was the only way that he would be able to face his family again, especially Breanna, who he assured that her honor would be avenged. This was surely going to break her heart.

Breanna was the one who sent them.

It was all her heart would be able to take to know she sent her brother and cousin to their deaths. It was a reality that would forever haunt her.

"Game time," Remmy announced when the scene cleared out with the last QPD patrol unit following the van away and up the quiet street.

"We gon' wait till the rest of these nosey ass muthafuckas go back in their houses," said Daisy, smoking on a Black & Mild cigar to ease her nerves. She was still undecided on how she was going to play this out. Just play the cards how they were dealt. Go with the flow and try to capitalize from it.

All the spectators crowded around outside, across the street and from several front yards, lingered for a minute or two to talk amongst each other and slowly began to disperse.

Only one person, a middle aged Black woman, stood at the front door of the Williams' residence. Just behind her, another woman stood, the wife, Latrice, who then beckoned the other woman inside with a wave. She went in and shut the door behind her.

"She got company, y'all," said Daisy.

"Collateral damage," remarked Von without even a flicker of remorse in her voice.

"They won't expect it when we show up on their doorstep. Just go up there normal like and knock on the door. Soon as they answer…"

"Smooth sailin' from there," Von said, and Remmy nodded his head in silent agreement. Then, she gave the order to put their plan in motion, and Daisy started up the truck to do just that.

Meanwhile, Daisy said that she would be the one to gain entrance first. Then, she would alert them that the scene was secured once she saw to it that everybody in the house was accounted for.

"I'm goin' wit' you this time," said Remmy.

"Do I have to remind you what your presence would manifest, boogeyman?" said Daisy, and that got a chuckle from Von. They were always bickering like two lovers, but Daisy always got her way.

"One of these days, you gon' walk your pretty ass into some helluva trouble," Remmy said.

"That's what they make guns for, baby."

"But guns ain't always trustin'," he replied sharply.

She grinned. "Then that's what I got you for," said Daisy, as she brought the SUV to a halt outside the designated house in question. She then reached beneath her seat for her gun and tucked it behind her. Then, she opened the door and got out.

"It won't be long now," Von said to Ty, who sat anxiously next to her, bouncing his right knee. She reached over and placed a hand upon his right knee, and she said, "Patience. Focus."

"I wanna kill this nigga!" he said. On their way there, Remmy had given Ty his P89 pistol, and it was the only assurance he had to carry out his vengeance with when the time permitted him to do so.

"Your opportunity is near, Ty. It's comin'."

As Daisy made her way to the front door, she kept her head down, but her attentiveness was sharp. She only saw one person about four houses down. They were leaving the safety of their home for the car parked in the driveway out front. Daisy stepped up to the door and knocked casually.

Behind her in the truck, she could feel all three pairs of eyes watching her every move.

But then, she sensed someone else watching too — some unseen presence hidden in the night.

24

"Who is it?" a woman's voice called out from the other side of the door.

"It's Monica Windbush, ma'am. I'm a colleague of Ray's, and I was sent here to see to your well-being," Daisy lied, obviously playing her role without effort. Persuasion was her game, and she'd mastered it.

Moments later, the door opened, and there stood Latrice Willimas, dressed in a pair of slacks and a cotton blouse. The look on her matured face was one of curiosity and caution.

"Ray never mentioned a Monica Windbush," she said.

"You are in danger, Latrice, and I'm only asking you to let me in the house. Don't look. But there's some people in the truck behind me wit' guns, and they came here to kill you, ma'am."

"Me?" Latrice gasped. "Kill me? Why?"

"Shhh, don't panic. I can help you. All you gotta do is let me come inside," said Daisy.

After a moment of caution, the woman stepped aside, and Daisy hurriedly stepped past her. Then, the front door was shut, and the game began.

***

The hospital room was quiet with an intense silence after Ray had retold his version of the story where Avery's murderous rage had taken two lives.

Prior to doing this, he had asked Coach Thompson and the reappearing Geno to leave the room. He wanted to speak with the mothers and the family, but Marolyn's presence was the exception. Tami made it clear that she was not to leave, that she was considered family to them now.

That endearment overwhelmed the woman.

Marolyn was grateful.

As for Geno, he was doing too much, and his actions had begun to draw untrust in the group. Lisa was tempted to cuss his ass out.

Then, Ray's cell phone rang, and he excused himself to the bathroom adjacent to the room. But before he could shut the door all the way, Tami forced her way inside behind him.

"Take your call," she said. Then, she stepped over to the commode and dropped her pants and panties to sit down and relieve herself.

Ray looked at her in surprise, the audacity of her. Then, he turned his back on Tami and answered his call. "Talk to me, Frank."

"Got some interestin' news for you, Ray," said Detective Franklyn Grant, the current lead detective investigating the deaths of Mane and those of Flip and his slaughtered crew.

"Give it to me, brotha."

"I reviewed the camera footage at the 24-Hour Kelly Jr. gas station where Mane Lofton's Dodge Charger was found and reported it through one of our contacts. Anyway, sir," said Frank, "the video shows Mane gettin' into a black Land Rover along wit' two other individuals. And guess who they were?"

"I hate guessin' games," said Ray.

"Daisy Herring and Remerald Scott."

The two names didn't register right away, but when it did, Ray felt his heart skip a beat. Then, a visual of Von Roberts appeared in his mind's eye, the stone-cold killer he knew that she was, but he could never seem to get his hands on her.

Years ago, when he was lead detective investigating the double-homicide of Bear Jones and Peanut Gaines, he was partners with Frank. The incident took place at the local Platinum Club, and two females were said to have caused so much hell about it that they had to shut the club down. Those two females were Daisy and Von, who shattered the night with Draco machine-guns after learning of Bear and Peanut having been killed outside the club. But when Ray finally did catch up with the pair afterwards — they didn't leave Quincy until they got answers — it was Von who he targeted with his scare tactics since she seemed the more aggressive.

Intimidation was a no-go with her.

Von was beyond moved.

Her reputation was bulletproof for a young eighteen-year-old female. She was seasoned.

"Another person was occupying the truck, but the video failed to identify them," Frank added, snatching Ray out of his troubled thoughts.

"It gotta be Von." Ray would bank his pension on that.

"Right," said Frank. "I think so too."

"If Daisy was there, then Von is close."

Frank also added that a witness spotted the Land Rover in the area around the same time gunshots were heard coming from Flip's house.

"So, there's a possibility they're Flip's killers too. Put an APB out on that SUV, Frank."

"Already done."

Ray glanced over at Tami and saw her perched on the lid of the toilet, watching him. He looked away from her and tuned back into his conversation with Frank.

"Oh, shit, Frank. It just hit me!"

"What?"

A worried look appeared on Tami's face when she saw the color drain from Ray's face.

"Vincent Roberts. Von's daddy. He was attacked on the job some hours ago by Avery Battles. Drove an ink pen right through the man's eye socket, and now he's in a coma over at TMH."

"Jesus," Frank whistled. "So, you think she's here for whoever this Avery Battles is?"

"No doubt in my mind, Frank," he answered.

"Is he one of yours?"

"Yeah."

"Then it's top priority."

"No, Frank," said Ray. "It's top priority whenever Von shows up anywhere on the radar."

27

When Ray finally hung up with his old partner, Tami rose up to her feet. She reached out and touched his arm, seeing that he was obviously troubled over whatever it was that filled his mind.

"Ray," she said slowly, "who is Von?"

When he looked at her, he could also see the worried expression on her face.

"Who is she?" Tami repeated.

With a big, exasperated breath, he told her what she wanted to know.

"And now that him and Rayneshia are together, that puts them both in danger," Ray replied once Tami had the full scoop on the situation.

"Then you got a real mission on your hands, Ray. It's time for you to go," she said. "Your children need you more than anything right now."

He nodded and turned for the door.

"And Ray?"

He looked back at her.

"I forgive you," Tami told him.

He said, "I won't let you down, Tam."

"Don't tell me what the hell you won't do," she replied in earnest. "Do what you gotta do."

That was all the encouragement Ray needed to get out of there and back into his Impala SS. Then, he peeled away from the hospital like a bat out of hell. Ray was scared for his daughter and Avery, knowing Von would not spare either one of them.

He was convinced Von would take pleasure in killing Rayneshia to hurt him.

His vendetta with her was real.

Von had to be stopped.

Thinking about the welfare of his family, Ray pulled out his phone to call his wife. He needed to know if she had heard from their daughter.

"Latrice," he replied when the phone was answered on the fourth ring.

A chuckle came over the line. "I bet you wish this was Latrice, huh, fuck boy?"

Ray damn near lost control of the car and crashed when he recognized the voice.

Von.

"Where is my wife?" he said after a few heartbeats.

"The same place you gon' be forever fuckin' wit' me," she said before the line disconnected.

And then total fear gripped his heart.

She had his wife.

His worst nightmare had now come to full bloom.

Ray cried. He was so frightened, he cried.

And that was when it happened.

The moment where nothing mattered except for the murder of Von Roberts once and for all.

Chapter 4

Cody was pulling on a fresh pair of socks when he sensed someone standing in the open doorway. He looked over and saw Rayneshia standing there. Every time he looked at her now, it disturbed him to see that they actually shared the same eyes. The last thing he'd ever expected was standing just in his bedroom doorway.

Then, Rayneshia let herself into the bedroom, and Cody stood up instinctively. He turned to face her, shirtless and eyes burning with soundless fury.

Suddenly, her curious facial expression transformed into a look of worry. Rayneshia brought herself closer to her brother and gaped down at the bruises along his body. She reached up to touch one, but Cody growled and took a cautious step back. Cody glared at his visible bruises then back up at her neck where bruises were just as pronounced.

"Avery said you had been shot earlier," she replied. Rayneshia saw him shaking, maybe out of boiling rage or because he was nervous, so she stepped around him to retrieve the fresh t-shirt he had lying on the bed. "You look like you're cold, little brotha." She handed him the shirt.

"Don't call me that shit," he said.

"Deal wit' it." Rayneshia turned away from him for the dresser top and mirror where his trophies and pictures were. She lifted up one of the football trophies and examined it while Cody quietly pulled on the clean shirt. Sitting it back where it was, Rayneshia ran her eyes over the photos he had spread around his dresser mirror.

"Was he really that bad to you?"

She turned around to face him. "Who? My daddy?" Rayneshia said and shrugged her well-toned shoulders. "He wasn't perfect."

"Nobody's perfect," he said

"He was never around enough." Rayneshia leaned back against the dresser and folded her arms over her luscious breasts. "Daddy was more devoted to his job than his family. It was as if he was purposefully neglecting his duty as a father and a husband. Like we were the problem when it really was him."

"So, him being a police detective got in the way of him being the person you and your mama needed him to be?"

"Ever since I can remember, yeah."

"No good memories at all?"

Right then, Bebop peeked around the corner of the doorway into the room. Cody looked at him and sneered, and Bebop ducked back out of sight.

Rayneshia pushed away from the dresser and moved over to sit on the edge of the bed. "He's great when he wants to be, Cody. He provides for us, and we want for nothing. All I can say is that he's capable of loving, and he's not the worst of men. You just have to push him more than you should," she said.

"A father shouldn't have to be forced to play his part."

"I totally agree, Cody."

"But what about you, Rayneshia? Who are you?"

"Me?" She pointed to herself.

He didn't answer her but instead stepped over to the bedroom closet for his Nike Air Maxes.

As she watched Cody step into his shoes, her gaze swiveled over to where the Air Jordans laid askew by the foot of the bed. Something came over her, as she studied the pair of shoes. Then, she leaned over to grab one of the shoes and held it up at eye level before something registered in her.

"These are brand new," said Rayneshia.

Cody said, "They're ruined now." He then stepped over to retrieve the shoe box the Jordans came in and asked her to put the shoe inside.

"Know what's so fuckin' strange, little brotha? Daddy went out and bought these same types of Air Jordans about five days ago."

Cody paused and stared at her.

"I was there when he brought them into the house. I actually snuck into his room while he was in the shower to investigate further." She appeared dreamy for a second or two. "Unfortunately, they weren't my size. They were size nine, two sizes more than mine."

Cody stiffened. "That's my size," he said. "I got those shoes this morning for my birthday today."

A smirk crossed her face.

"What?"

"Daddy bought you those shoes," she said.

"No!" Cody shook his head wearily.

"I believe so, little brotha. I don't believe in coincidences. The same shoes, the size, the relation between you and him. I have no doubt in my mind that they came from our father," exclaimed Rayneshia.

Without commenting, Cody snatched up the second shoe and stuffed it into the box. Then, he marched out of the room for the kitchen where he located a bottle of lighter fluid and some matches. A minute later, Cody was out the back door.

"What is he doing?" Kelli asked behind her friend's shoulder, as Rayneshia stood in the doorway of the back door, staring out after Cody.

Bebop slipped between them and leapt off the back porch to see what Cody was up to.

Behind the house was an old barbecue grill sitting underneath a large pine tree towering over the majority of the backyard. This was where Tami threw her special cookout parties when she was up to it.

Cody opened the top of the big grill and tossed the shoe box onto the grate. Then, he began to douse lighter fluid all over the box and shoes.

"You 'bout to burn your Jordans?" Bebop said this in astonishment. "Why?"

"They're bad luck," he answered.

"How?"

"They just is, Bebop. Stand back, lil brah!" Cody told him before striking a long stem match. Bebop glanced back at the girls with a shrug.

Woosh! That was the sound it made after the lit match was tossed into the grill. A sudden burst of fire flames enveloped the shoe box, as its force of heated pressure made them step back farther away.

They stood there watching it burn.

No words were needed.

Avery eventually appeared alongside Bebop and dropped an arm over his bony shoulders. He and Cody exchanged a knowing glance, and all Avery did was offer him a respective nod.

Cody said, "It was him that did it, not Mama. She lied to me once again."

"About what, brah?"

"The shoes."

Avery considered what he said. "Mr. Ray bought you the Jordans 12s?"

Cody nodded. "Yeah."

"But," Bebop interjected, "even tho' she told a story, she still made sure you got what you wanted for your birthday."

He was right. Regardless of who paid for the shoes, they were accomplished. Maybe Tami applied some pressure on Ray to step up to the plate. She had to because how else would he have known the exact model shoe and size?

"You dead ass right, lil' brah," Cody said to Bebop.

"But you still mad at Mama Tee?" said Bebop.

"Yep."

"But?" Avery replied.

At that instant, the back door of Alisha's house opened, and both Twan and Souljah stepped outside. The two loyal gangstas hurried over toward them. From the look of their urgent approach, Cody automatically knew something was very wrong.

"We got a serious problem, y'all," Twan said.

"All the problems we'd had t'night was serious," Cody replied in a sarcastic tone.

"Yeah, you right about that, Young C. But this bitch is on a whole other level. Her murder game is proper."

"What bitch?" asked Bebop curiously.

"The same bitch who has come all the way here to kill you, Av." Twan was looking dead in Avery's eyes when he said this.

"W-Who?" Avery blurted out.

"Her name is Vontoria," said Souljah.

Vontoria? thought Avery, puzzled. He didn't know anybody by that name at all.

But he damn sure was about to find out.

***

It only took Daisy a full minute to explain the tremendous dangers that awaited them outside to get Latrice and her sister, Sophia, to act on her terms.

"Any second now, they'll be in here, and everybody in this house will be dead," said Daisy, hoping against hope that she made it out alive herself.

"But Avery is not here anymore," said Latrice.

Daisy blinked. "He's not?"

"He snuck out through the back a little over an hour ago." Latrice didn't trust herself to include Rayneshia because she didn't know where that would lead to.

"Please don't lie to me," Daisy warned her.

"I'm not," cried the detective's wife.

"She's tellin' the truth," Sophia replied. She was a well-fit woman who looked like she could move fast and swiftly if need be.

Why would they lie when they could just easily give Avery up to save themselves? Daisy hated to believe it, but it was true. Latrice offered to prove just that in a panic, but Daisy declined the opportunity. Instead, she ushered the two women toward the back door where they escaped.

A destination wasn't decided, only that they needed to get out of there fast.

Those killas were on the way.

That was seven minutes ago, and Von was at her very end with patience, Remmy too, who sat anxiously in the front seat, repeatedly checking his watch.

"What the fuck!?" he replied in agitation.

Von didn't like the feeling she was getting. Daisy should have alerted them by now. She glanced over at Ty, and his hand rested on the door handle. He was ready to make a muthafucker bleed.

"Vee?" Remmy looked back at her.

Reluctantly, Von sighed deeply and said, "Fuck it. Let's go! Daisy's in there. I'm all in!" With that being said, she opened the door and got out.

Remmy was out of the truck before her feet even touched the ground.

"Full speed ahead, lil brah," said Remmy to Ty, and Ty just nodded in response.

When Remmy took off for the front door of the house, Ty followed suit. Taking the rear of the train of force was Von, who now clutched two Beretta pistols in each hand. Her focus was on her immediate surroundings just in case someone was lying in wait in the shadows for them.

No one dared to reveal themselves. No pressure.

But then, pressure came. Remmy charged the front door full force, and with one vicious right foot kick, the door exploded inwardly, and he entered like a raging fullback. The three of them moved with natural precision, as they invaded the home.

The only sound that welcomed them was a Donald Trump skit playing on the WCTV Channel 6 News on the wide-screen TV in the spacious living room. Von watched as Ty and Remmy went about searching the house. She didn't want to exercise the thought, but for some reason, she believed no one was even in the house.

Remmy and Ty were tearing up the place.

Other than the TV and now their whirlwind of destructive behavior, the house was eerily silent. Where had everybody gone? Where was Daisy? And what the hell did all this mean?

The sudden ring of a cell phone startled Von, and she looked in its direction. The smartphone was sitting on top of the glass coffee table in the middle of the living room floor.

"Ain't nobody here," said Remmy breathlessly, appearing in the doorway of the great big room.

Von held up a finger, as she picked up the ringing cell phone. "It's Ray," she said and answered the phone, knowing this was the moment she would put absolute fear in the heart of the big bad detective.

"Latrice?" he replied.

Von chuckled evilly in the phone. "I bet you wish this was Latrice, huh, fuck boy?" she hissed into the phone like a venomous cobra.

"Where is my wife?" Ray demanded.

He knows it's me, thought Von grimly. "The same place you gon' be forever fuckin' wit' me," she told him and sent him straight to the dial tone. Then, she slipped the phone into her pants pocket and looked up to find Ty missing. "Where's Ty?"

Looking around them and noticing Ty wasn't there, Remmy frowned and turned back for the hallway with Von on his heels.

They found Ty standing out back on the doorstep, gazing into the night.

"They hit the back door on us," said Ty.

"Yeah," Von replied. "I see that, Ty." Then, she put the Beretta to the back of his head and sent two slugs pushing out the front of his face.

Ty was dead before he hit the ground.

"Let's go," she said.

Twenty seconds later, they were back in the SUV and speeding down the street.

Meanwhile, Remmy was questioning Von's actions back at the house and whether Daisy had somehow double-crossed him and Von.

As they distanced themselves from the crime scene, Von was surfing through Latrice's cell phone and using her own phone to document the information she was receiving. "That other bitch was Latrice's sista, Sophia Greene," she muttered knowledgeably.

"What do you think happened wit' Dee?" he asked.

"Daisy went against the grain."

The statement sounded so absurd that Remmy wasn't sure he should take her seriously.

"I sensed somethin' about her after we burned Avery's house up," said Von. "She seemed nervous, kept checkin' her phone; I noticed her on the phone the second I stepped out the door. But by the time we was back inside the truck, she had the phone sittin' between her legs as if she was never on it."

"What about that shit she pulled back at the hospital?" he asked. "About going in there alone?"

"It was all game, Remmy."

"Why?"

"I don't know why exactly," she said. "But you know Daisy is originally from here in Quincy?"

"Real shit?"

"Real shit."

"Where at exactly?"

That made Von frown. "Shaw Quarters."

There was no reply from Remmy. He was taking all of it in. He had only been part of their team for about a year now. Daisy had been there since day one, and it was her who decided to bring him aboard. Remmy considered Daisy family, the sister he never had. Now, her latest act had caused him to look at her in a very dark light.

Why was Daisy protecting them? Avery? What was her relation to him? He had to be important to risk betraying their trust.

"Could it be she's some kin to the lil' nigga?" he just had to ask. Remmy's brain was reeling in all types of shit right now, and he wasn't liking the areas in which his mind was taking him.

"It's a possibility."

"And if it's not what we're assumin'?"

Von was quiet for a long minute. "She still dies," she replied. "Because all you need is one chance to make me distrust you, even if it's just a misconception. You only get one shot wit' Vontoria."

Chapter 5

Speaking of which, Daisy had been staring out the window of the dark bedroom of the house next door. She knew they were coming for her before long. Daisy had watched them invade Latrice's house then waited for the outcome of their findings.

Before his death, Ty had come outside on the back porch. He searched the night for them. Then, he looked toward the house and directly at the window Daisy was looking out of. He stared at the very window for a long time. Daisy would have sworn that he saw her in the window, and she stepped back out of the way. Her heart was beating like a marching band bass drum.

Then, Remmy and Von came through the back door, and to Daisy's astonishment, knowing how deadly Von was, she blew Ty's brains out the front of his head. That sight was one to behold.

It symbolized Daisy's own fate.

Her betrayal.

And that was when she called Rikah and told her what she had done.

"So, you can consider her a threat to you now," said Rikah with an ice-cold tone of voice. "Which means if she can't get you…"

"She'll go after those I love," Daisy said. She'd known Von far too long not to know her habits and the way she thought. She knew Von so well that she could take her face off and put it on her own, and no one would tell the difference. She knew her behavioral patterns and had learned and practiced them numerous times.

"Now we beat her to the punch," said Rikah.

"What're you gonna do?"

"Just leave it up to me, lil cuz. I got'chu. And to be real wit'chu, I've been waitin' on this opportunity for a long time now."

"Really, girl?"

"Yeah."

"But you never told me nothin'."

Rikah figured with someone like Von, with that much power and respect in the streets, it would one day get to her head. That she would feel so untouchable that she thought she could cross out anybody and get away with it. Rikah knew with Daisy being so close to Von, it was a sure thing Von would cross her out, that she would consider Daisy a liability because she knew too much.

Or maybe for some other personal unknown reason.

"I'll keep you posted, Daisy."

"After I'm done here, I'm coming home," Daisy said, meaning her old bedroom at Rikah's place in the gated community home she owned.

Rikah said, "About time."

The bedroom door opened, and there stood Latrice looking in on her.

"Can I come in?" she asked.

This whole time, Daisy had been sitting in the darkness of the bedroom. The house she was in was owned by Latrice's good friends, Marcus and Melissa Keaton, and the bedroom belonged to their daughter, Jazmyne, who was gone to the National Guard Corps.

"This isn't my place to deny you entry," said Daisy in a tired voice.

"But you're entitled to your own personal space."

"C'mon, Latrice. Damn," she said.

The woman entered the dark room but left the door open to let the light of the hallway pour in.

Daisy watched as the detective's wife pulled up a chair from the old computer desk across the room. She sat down across from Daisy and just stared at her for a long moment.

"Are you gonna say somethin' or just look at my gorgeous face all fuckin' day?"

"You Carlos Herring's daughter," said Latrice and got the expected reaction from Daisy. "I know your daddy well. But your mama, Kimberly Smart, now that was a helluva woman back in the day."

"What do you mean by that?" Daisy asked.

"Feisty. Smart. And beautiful like yourself. Kim and I were good friends back then."

"Was," said Daisy.

"The years make some people grow apart. You know. You moved away young, and it tore your mama to pieces. I remember. I wasn't always there wit' Kim, but I darn sure was there for her."

Daisy didn't say anything further to the woman. She got up and cut on the light. There was something about the woman's voice that struck a familiar chord in Daisy. She hadn't gotten the chance to actually really look at Latrice. The moments had been fleeting, and Daisy was too focused on watching what was going on around her.

"It'll come to you in due time," said Latrice, seeing how Daisy was looking at her.

But it had already registered, and Daisy found herself gaping at the woman in great surprise. It has been damn near thirteen years since she saw the woman who now sat before her.

"You were there at the hospital just before my daddy died," said Daisy.

"From that car wreck. Yes, I was."

"You the one who took me round to the gift shop in the hospital to buy something for my daddy. The same time my daddy died."

Latrice nodded. "He told her, your mama, that he felt it gettin' close and that he didn't want you to see him take his last breath. So, your mama asked me to take you away." As Latrice said this, there were tears in her eyes, and suddenly, Daisy felt overwhelmed by the old emotions.

She was still affected by that loss. Daisy had loved and cherished her father. She was just sixteen when Carlos Herring died in that hospital. Five months later, she killed the father of the drunk driver who took her father away from her.

"I know all about what you were going through that day, Daisy," whispered Latrice.

No reply.

It's a small world, thought Daisy. Small town. So small that everybody knew one another or were friends at one point in time.

Before Daisy could allow herself to grow sad about her father's passing, her cautionary instinct clicked on when the sound of Ray Williams' car engine came roaring down the street. Then, from somewhere up front, Sophia called out to her sister to inform her that Ray had finally arrived.

"Don't worry yourself," said Latrice to Daisy after noticing the look on her face. "I will tell Ray that you saved our lives this morning. And he will protect you, Daisy. I know he would."

Daisy watched the detective's wife hurry out of the room, and she was right behind her. But Daisy was moving in the opposite direction from where Latrice was headed to meet her husband.

Seeing Ray was out of the question.

And he couldn't protect her.

Not from Von.

So straight back for the back door she went. Daisy glanced over her shoulder and saw Marcus Keaton watching her but said nothing. The man would rather have her gone than being there.

Outside, Daisy didn't even look left where she knew Ty laid dead in the dirt. She went right through the neighboring backyards and disappeared.

Now the hunt began.

Not that she was afraid or anything, but Daisy needed to watch her every step where Von's cruel intentions were concerned. She was a killer too, and Von was evidently aware of how merciless Daisy could also be. She had more bodies under her belt than Von. Von was just a different kind of creature that shouldn't be underestimated.

Daisy knew her weakness though.

Every killer had one.

Or more. And Von knew hers very well.

***

It was then that Cody told Rayneshia that she should go back home. Rayneshia wasn't trying to hear him, but after Rod pulled her aside and spoke with her, whatever he said was enough to change her mind about staying around.

Cody was restrapping the bulletproof vest around him when Rayneshia reappeared back in the bedroom where Avery was conferring with him. "Can I have a second wit' my little brotha, Av, before I go?" she said.

Avery looked over at Cody, and Cody nodded his head reluctantly. He had been in the process of preparing himself for war and checking the clip of the .9mm Ruger that Cody had taken from his mother's bedroom dresser. He set the gun aside on the bed and left the room without argument.

He didn't want to leave Cody's sight.

Protectiveness.

When Avery was gone, it was then that Rayneshia wrapped her arms around Cody. Her sudden, unexpected affection caught him off guard. Cody stood there awkwardly. Her tight embrace was hurting him, but he didn't say anything.

"I know we just met each other, Cody, but you are my only sibling, and I love you," she stated before releasing him. When he looked at her, Cody saw tears in her eyes. "You better not die on me, little brotha. I swear I'll never forgive you."

"Who said anythang about dying?"

"I know what's going on," said Rayneshia. "I know what's about to go down out there."

"Go home, Rayneshia."

She hesitated. "Put it on everythang you love, you'll be absolutely careful out there."

"Rayneshia," he was about to admonish her.

"Do it, Cody!" she whined

With a long, frustrated sigh, he did what she asked of him. Then, she pulled him back in her arms, squeezing the breath out of him.

After Rayneshia left, Bebop came trudging in the room, looking like he'd lost his best friend.

"Don't gimme that look, little brah. You know you're not comin' wit' us. It's too dangerous." Cody had pulled over another shirt to cover the vest.

"I'm not scared," Bebop told him.

"I said no, Bebop."

"But I got this," the boy persisted, and then he pulled out a small compact .380 automatic pistol from his front pocket.

This really surprised Cody, and he glared down at his little crony. "Where'd you get that?"

"I took it from somebody."

"From who?" It was one thing seeing Bebop with a gun in his hand but another thing knowing Bebop would also use it too. But he didn't take it from him. Cody was not going to be petty about it.

"I took it from Roe from around the corner. I saw him one day stash it…"

"I don't even wanna know, Bebop." Cody couldn't believe Bebop stole the gun from Roe, who was one of the hustlas in the neighborhood and who'd also shoot you in a heartbeat.

Twan then appeared in the bedroom doorway to ask Cody if he was ready to ride. Then, he spotted the gun in Bebop's hand and frowned.

"What you doin' wit' that gun, jit?" Twan stepped fully into the room.

"Somebody gotta stay back and protect the rest of the neighborhood while y'all gone."

"And you think you ready for that responsibility?" replied Twan amusingly.

Bebop nodded solemnly. "I'm born ready."

"I'm on my way, Twan," said Cody. "Lemme finish up wit' Bebop right quick." Twan exited the room, and Cody turned his undivided attention on the boy, as Bebop dared not cower under his piercing gaze. "You are my little brotha always, Bebop."

"I know that already, Cody."

But what Cody shared with him next, Bebop didn't know. Though the boy was sure that what he was being told was for his own benefit. Then, he spun on his heels and marched out the door with the gun still clutched in his hand.

He had a new attitude.

Bebop was proudful.

And Cody hoped like hell he didn't just set his little brotha up to be another victim.

When the time came, the crew hopped back into traffic with two more stolen cars Yak had provided for them.

All except for Menace, who was left knocked out cold in Alisha's bed. He was too injured and emotionally unbalanced to go to war. And he was going to be one mad muthafucker if he woke up again and found them all gone.

And they could use his treacherousness if he hadn't gotten himself shot out there. Pity.

Money Mel, Avery, and Cody were riding in a burgundy-colored Infiniti with Po'Boy at the wheel. Their mission was to find Von and her kill team before she found them and at least try to kill Avery. Meanwhile, Twan and his team were headed out to Tallahassee to try and cover grounds on getting the advantage on Von there. It was understood that Von was more of a threat than Lank and Lil Earl, who they all knew were also probably entertaining the thought of retaliation.

Po'Boy had seen it all and had heard it all, but he wasn't convinced Lank would let the situation go. With Rontay probably dead by now and Lank being forced in a corner, who else would he direct his growing rage at?

Retaliation was a must.

Everybody had reason to believe if they didn't play according to the rules of war, there was a big possibility they wouldn't survive.

"She's smart enough to know that truck she's ridin' in is hot by now," said Money Mel. He had just received a text from Twan informing him that his source claimed there was an APB out on the truck Von was said to be occupying.

"And didn't Twan say the other girl she's wit' name is Daisy?" asked Avery.

Po'Boy affirmed it.

The question had really been Cody's, but Avery decided to voice it instead. The name sounded so familiar to him, but he couldn't quite pinpoint it.

"I know Daisy," said Money Mel. "That's what I've been meaning to run across you anyway, Cody, when Twan and 'em first mentioned them bitches."

"Why you wanted to run it 'cross me?" Cody asked.

"Because," said Money Mel, "if I'm not mistaken, Daisy is some kin to you."

"What?" Cody and Avery said in unison.

"I talked to my mama again t'night," Money Mel replied. "She told me about Daisy showin' up not that long ago and was concerned about her visit. Apparently, Daisy hasn't come home in years, and now all of a sudden, she's in the hospital askin' questions. Y'all know how Mama is. Always distrustin' and cautious about everythang. Anyway, the Daisy I know has a cousin named Rikah, and Rikah is the wifey of my connect. I met him through her, and that's how I remember Daisy, lil' brah."

"Torikah Taylor?"

"Yeah," nodded Money Mel. "That's her."

"Damn," muttered Po'Boy. "I know her. She's originally from Shaw Quarters. And Daisy too. Wasn't it her old man that died all them years ago?"

"From a car accident, I think."

"The streets were tryna say that Daisy had been the one who offed that old cracker in Havana."

"That's what they said." Money Mel explained to Cody and Avery what they were referring to. "The old white man was the son of the dude who killed Daisy's daddy in that car wreck," he said.

"What is Daisy's mama name?" asked Cody. Something was trying to reach out to him, something he hadn't thought about in a very long time.

"I don't know, can't remember. But I'm about to hit Rikah up right now and see what the play is," said Money Mel, and he hit his connect up on speed dial.

Avery glanced over at his brotha. "Why would Daisy want to hurt me if she knows…"

"She doesn't know," said Cody. "If she really is my cousin, she doesn't know you my brotha. Don't worry, Av. We gon' get to the bottom of it."

47

Chapter 6

When Detective Ray Williams stepped through the back door of his house, he came to an instant halt. He breathed in the fresh morning air as dawn approached, smelling death and losing another shattered piece of his sanity. Ray took another step forward and then another, bringing himself closer to the dead body.

Ten minutes ago, he had pulled up out front with his Glock in his hand. The first thing he saw was the front door hanging open. Ray's heart squeezed with fear, as he began to charge for the house. Then, just before he reached the first step, he heard Sophia call out to him from next door. It was then that he saw his beloved wife and her sister standing upon the doorstep of the house next door.

Ray wanted to cry at that point. The relief hit him like a punch to the chest.

"What happened? Where is Neshia? I thought…" Ray had to catch his breath, as Latrice ran smack into him and damn near made him tumble over onto the ground. Crying her heart out, Latrice went about telling him of her terrifying experience.

"She did what?!" Ray was shocked by what he had heard Daisy had done to save his family.

Von did not like this part of the game. He dwelled on the matter at hand. Ray, although he knew that he shouldn't, because he knew Daisy was a murderer, he couldn't wait to see her and tell her how grateful he was of her doing what she did.

Unfortunately, there was no more wrong Daisy could do in his eyes.

Daisy had earned a new ally.

Then, Ray was told about the body behind the house and hurried over to see it for himself. He knew that it was Tyler before he could see his face. He knew the young man had somehow cliqued up with Von and had come back for Avery after what was done to his brother and cousin.

The very same people he trusted were the ones that murdered him.

"Von." He automatically knew it was her who took Ty's life. Von was mad at what Daisy had done and wanted to release her rage out on someone.

Ty fell victim to her rage.

Not wanting to disturb the crime scene, Ray backed away from the body and whipped out his phone. He then called the incident in just two seconds before the first patrol unit showed up. Somebody had already called it in, Ray was informed by dispatch.

Within the next twenty minutes, his home was once again crawling with CSI officials and this time, Chief Kelvin Moore. The chief was not happy one bit, and he didn't need to tell Ray before he could see it.

"If Donnie was alive right now, what the hell do you think he'd do to you right this second, Ray?" said the chief. At the thought of the former chief of police, the late Donald Goodman and Moore's predecessor, a shiver ran up Ray's spine.

And that was when Chief Moore drew back and punched him hard in the chest, knocking the breath out of him.

"That's what he would do," snarled the older, bigger man, daring Ray to challenge him.

At the doorway of the large den area stood Latrice with two mugs of coffee in her hands. When she saw the physical interaction, she already knew what had transpired between both men.

"Donnie would then revisit words he'd already told you before where his daughter's well-being is concerned. So, this is what I'm gonna tell you in my own words, Ray Williams," said Chief Moore grudgingly.

Latrice turned and walked away.

"You better not fuck up, or so help me God, I'm gonna kill you my damn self. Now get the fuck out my face and go catch our killers!" the chief growled.

Biting his bottom lip to keep from spazzing out on his boss, Ray nodded quietly, but there was no denying the fire in his eyes.

"Oh. I see. You wanna fight me now?" said the chief, seeing that killer in his eyes.

Ray didn't reply.

Before he lost his mind and pushed the chief's nose bone up into his brain, killing him where he stood, Ray turned away from him. He walked back toward the front, past his colleagues, his wife, and Sophia and headed straight for the door.

"Daddy." Rayneshia was the first person he saw the moment he stepped outside.

"You got some explaining to do, young lady," he replied before opening out his arms to her. "I'm glad you are alright though. You had us worried."

"I know, Daddy," said Rayneshia.

He looked at her.

"I met Cody," she replied. Rayneshia saw him flinch, and that was the reaction she expected.

"Where is he? Where's Avery?" Ray took his daughter by the arm and pulled her out of earshot of the coming and going of the officials through the front door. Kelli also stood a few yards off to allow them to talk more privately. "Neshia, where are they?"

"I know where they were but not now."

"But you was wit' them?"

"Didn't I say I just met my brotha?" Her tone was snappish, and Ray shrugged with acceptance.

"Tell me what you know."

"Everything," she said.

He waited.

And she told him all about what she witnessed while in the company of Avery, her brotha, and the others. This was what Ray was afraid of, his daughter being exposed to the likes of street dudes. But little did he know, she was in a serious relationship with one — one that he would definitely not approve of.

"Okay." Ray was dizzy with adrenaline and shaken with fear of what was to become. "Your mother and Aunt Sophia is inside. Go in and keep them company but please stay outta the way, Rayneshia."

"You don't have to tell me," said Rayneshia. "You're the one who brought trouble home to us."

Before he could say anything further, Rayneshia hurried away from him. He watched as she hooked her arm through Kelli's, and together, they slowly entered through the front door of the house.

"Sarge?" a voice called out to him.

Turning at the voice, Ray saw that it was Detective Sharon Eddison approaching him from the curb where her Ford Mustang was parked across the street.

"Sharon, what the hell are you doing here?" he demanded aggressively, eyeing his partner and reaching out to her to steady her on her feet.

"Chad called and filled me in on everything," said the white, blonde headed woman detective who had been Ray's partner for the past two years now. Detective Eddison was supposed to be on maternity leave after just having her first child a month ago. Then, she punched him on the arm and said, "You could've at least called and told me something."

"I didn't wanna worry you."

"Selfish, selfish." Sharon clicked her teeth twice.

"Sharon, I can't ask you to be involved in this — at least not this one. It's a very personal one, and it's too very dangerous for you."

"Dangerous is my middle name, Ray."

"No," he shook his head.

"I'm not…"

"Woman, I said no! No. I must do this alone. Please don't fight me about this, Sharon, please. Go back home and care for your little son," he begged her. "Go do that."

"So you can care for your son? Right, Ray?"

Ray stiffened.

"Don't act like you're surprised I know, Ray. Remember I'm a detective. It's why you took me under your wing. I detect shit most people try to hide," Detective Eddison said with a straight face.

"How long have you known?" he asked.

"Almost as long as we've been partners."

"Damn," he muttered. "I'm slippin'."

"No, Ray. I'm good." Sharon patted him on the shoulder just as his cell phone rang.

Ray reached into his coat pocket for the phone and fished out the device. When he saw the number he didn't recognize, Ray felt a premonition of dread wash over him at that moment.

"Hello? Who is this?" answered Ray in a shaky voice that Sharon detected instantly.

"It's your worst nightmare, nigga," said the voice on the other end of the phone.

Von. He swallowed nervously.

And that was when he heard the gunshot. The bullet zoomed past his face. And then, there was the unmistakable thunk of the bullet's impact striking its mark. Blood splattered along the side of Ray's face. He looked down and couldn't believe his eyes.

Detective Sharon Eddison laid at his feet, twitching as death closed in on her, with a large hole in her head.

The twitching stopped.
Dead.
And then, Ray screamed.

***

From between the two houses up the street about fifty yards away, Remmy smirked in satisfaction at delivering the perfect headshot. Then, he tucked the M24 sniper's rifle, turned on his heels, and darted through the shadows back the way he had come. Remmy was fast on his feet, way too fast to be caught from the distance.

Two blocks away, Von sat behind the wheel of a black Dodge Challenger. She heard Ray's sharp intake of breath through the phone, then the man screamed bloody murder, and it was music to her ears.

That was another thing Von was good at. Playing mind games. Driving others to insanity.

She knew the detective would eventually show up at his house after giving him quite the scare when she answered his wife's phone. It didn't hit Von until after she had stolen the car that she should target Ray some more. Von wanted for sure action. Finding Avery and the others was proving to be difficult.

She needed to quench her crave for more blood but from those with who she personally begrudged.

And Remmy, who too was longing for a shot to shed some blood of his own, was relieved when Von shared her wicked thoughts with him. Remmy had a goodie bag with an assortment of weapons that he could choose from. The rifle came in as handy as it always had during previous missions. All Von said was to make the detective hurt but not to kill him. Remmy saw a good opportunity and took his shot.

And Ray Williams was definitely hurting.

It made her smile.

Minutes later, she spotted Remmy hurrying in her direction along the street. She didn't see the M24 rifle because Remmy had broken it down into its several pieces while he fled. The rifle was now contained inside the backpack he carried on his back.

"Beautiful," Von said the moment he opened the door and slid into the seat beside her.

"I took out his partner," said Remmy.

"The woman?"

He nodded.

Another dead cop, thought Von. That would no doubt make things sticky, but she loved it.

Before he could fire up the pre rolled blunt Von had prepared for them, she started up the car and got the hell out of Friendship. She took the back roads out and made it safely back in town.

"Remember that scenario Daisy pointed out to us earlier about the old girl at the hospital?" Remmy said this through a mouthful of weed smoke.

"About snatchin' her up?"

"Yeah, but not that way in particular," he said and passed her the blunt.

"Whateva you're about to say, don't say it. The hospital is too risky. Plus, we got Daisy to worry about, Remmy," said Von. "She knows how we think, so to get her, we'll have to switch it up."

"Okay."

"We gotta stay ten steps ahead of her."

Remmy hesitated before speaking. "How we gonna do that, Von?" he asked.

Von was coming upon the subdivision area and turned onto the side road between the old IGA grocery store and General Electric and passed the old railroad crossing. She drove past the old Carol's Diner and bust a quick left at the second turn.

"We gotta assume Dee has somehow contacted the others, and they're congregatin' somewhere to plot on us. So, what we're gonna do is get the hell outta Quincy and lay low."

"So, we're running?" said Remmy.

"Hell no!"

"Then, what are we doing, Von?"

"Restrategizin'."

"Sounds like runnin' to me." But what Remmy really wanted to say was was Von afraid of Daisy now that she was playing for the other side? But he kept his mouth shut on that note, knowing that he wouldn't live afterwards.

Then, Von's phone rang, and she retrieved it from her lap. It was a video call from her mother's number, and Von answered it immediately.

"What's up, Ma?" she replied.

At first, the images on the screen were a little fuzzy. Then, it cleared, and Von saw what laid before her eyes.

"Which one should die first?" a voice spoke from somewhere beyond the other phone.

On the screen was an image of Von's mother, Sonya, and her girl, Reyzyne, both bound and gagged and staring up into the screen pleadingly. At this vision, Von felt a bubble of fear swell up in her chest, making it hard for her to breathe.

Remmy looked over at the screen, and all he could do was shake his head sadly.

"You want me," Vontoria "Von" Roberts said, glaring at the screen.

"You know how the game goes."

Rikah. Von frowned when she recognized the other voice.

"So, this how we're playin' it, Rikah?" she said with malice laden in her tone.

"I play the cards how they're dealt, Von."

"Then you won't get me like that, boo. Do what you do," said Von menacingly. "Just know it'll be my move next," she threatened.

"So, you're sacrificing your family?"

Von laughed deliriously. "Bitch, when have you ever known me to have a muthafuckin' heart?"

"That's bad, Von. You have no honor," Rikah told her.

"Nah, ho, it just got worse," said Von and disconnected the communication and tossed the phone aside. "Where that muthafuckin' weed at?!"

Remmy passed it over.

And Von hit that bitch like it was the last muthafucka left.

Chapter 7

If there was one person that Daisy could trust at that moment, it was BJ Harris from Havana. Of course, there were plenty others that she could have chosen from, but BJ and her shared something more profound.

Daisy had eventually made it all the way back to the two o'clock BP gas station without incident. It was closed and would soon be opening now that dawn was nearing. But BJ would be there to scoop her up before then, she hoped.

Meanwhile, Daisy remained hidden in the shadows alongside the building's structure. The only person that shared the space with her was a gray bearded homeless man lying inside of his makeshift cardboard residence asleep. Daisy glanced in his direction but didn't disturb him from his sleep.

By now, BJ should be halfway there to retrieve her. When she had phoned him, BJ sounded as though he was already up and about. He assured her that he was on his way at that very moment.

To know that BJ had her back made Daisy feel a lot better despite her circumstances.

Where Von assumed her and BJ's acquaintance as established a year ago after Von introduced them, it was way before that night in the L&J's Lounge in Havana. Their bond told a story that began ten years prior.

Daisy had accumulated all the information she needed on Thomas "Tommy Boy" Hansen, the white guy who had drunkenly been responsible for her father's death. Tommy Boy was then in custody, facing a vehicular homicide charge, and later received ten years for his fault. But since Daisy couldn't get to Tommy Boy, she aimed her vengeance toward his father instead, William "Han-Man" Hansen. One night while her mother was asleep, Daisy had stolen her father's old .22 revolver and hitchhiked all the way to Rich Bay, Havana where she'd learned Han-Man lived. It was 2:00 in the morning when she walked right up to the front door of the Hansen's residence and knocked on the door. Where she had expected the old white man to answer, it was his wife that came to the door.

"Back the fuck up, bitch!" Daisy drew down on the old, liver spotted, white lady and put the .22 right in her wrinkled face.

The woman gasped and reached for her heart in obvious fright of being shot.

Daisy shoved her in the chest, and the woman stumbled backwards and tumbled onto the floor. Knowing that she had to make this quick because the old man was said to be an army veteran, Daisy didn't take any chances of allowing Han-Man to get the upper hand.

"Stay right there or I swear I'll shoot your ass," said Daisy to the woman before stepping over her to go in search of her husband.

Han-Man Hansen was lying in bed, assisted by an oxygen tube inserted into his nostrils. When Daisy entered the room, she found the old man awake and staring back at her in confusion. His lips moved, but Daisy couldn't hear what he was saying. No words were convincing enough to talk her out of doing what she came to do. Daisy walked up to the bed and glared down at the man who she saw was dying already. But in her eyes, he was a killer — she saw Tommy Boy in his father. And that was evidence enough to make her lift the .22 and place it against his thick, bushy eyebrow.

"I forgive... you," said Han-Man, and Daisy looked at him in silent loathe.

She squeezed the trigger, killing him. Hot tears ran down her face. Then, she turned around and dashed for the door and back through the house where the man's wife was still lying on the floor.

"I don't wanna die," said Martha Hansen, crying and scared to death when Daisy suddenly skidded to a stop and aimed the gun at her next. Daisy was smart enough to know that in order for her to get away scot-free, she couldn't leave any witnesses.

She pulled the trigger.

Nothing.

Daisy pulled the trigger again.

Click.

Click. Click.

Frowning, Daisy stared down at the old woman, who stared back up at her in fear. Then, Daisy sneered and drew back and went across the woman's head with the gun. The impact sent her crashing to the floor and unconscious.

Having believed that she'd served her purpose, Daisy then took off running for the door. But she didn't get far before she stumbled down the porch steps and lost her footing. When Daisy hit the ground, the gun discharged, and there was a burning, hot, painful sensation in her right leg. Her upper thigh hurt like hell, as the thought of being shot scared her. Then, panic overwhelmed her, as Daisy painfully struggled to her feet and limped away from the scene.

That was when BJ showed up just as she made it halfway up the road. He suddenly appeared out of nowhere, and Daisy pointed the gun at him. Then, her leg gave out on her, and Daisy tilted off balance and was falling, and BJ rushed in to catch her. She was caught in between trying to catch herself and defending herself from the boy who'd unexpectedly showed up.

"I got'chu, Daisy," he said, throwing one of her arms across his shoulders to keep her balanced.

"How you know me?" she winced.

*"Just hurry up and let's go before somebody catches us,"
BJ told her, as he then led the way with her struggling
alongside him and trying not to cry out in pain for fear of
embarrassing herself further than how she did back at the
house.*

*That night, BJ led her to his house where he lived two
streets over. It was there, in his bathroom tub, where he
coaxed Daisy out of her black sweatpants to examine her
bullet wound. It turned out to be a deep gash where the bullet
had grazed her thigh and had it bleeding like crazy. BJ went
about tending to her wound and making Daisy cry in spite of
her fight to stay calm. Right there in his bathroom, BJ made
a true friend out of Daisy that would last for many years
ahead.*

"You know me?" Daisy asked him later.

*"You're Rikah's cousin," he said and added that he went
to school with Rikah, that he was a few years older than her,
and his acquaintance with Rikah was only due to the same
circle that they ran in. "You lucky I saw you when I did,"
said BJ with a tone of earnestness that made her wonder, and
BJ decided to fill her in on how he came to being there to
save her from being caught.*

*BJ had just exited from the house where his girlfriend,
Pumpkin, lived when Daisy was let out at the corner. He
recognized her from the moment the dome light in the car
illuminated her features, and when she walked beneath the
glow of the streetlight at the corner, he sensed she was up to
something for her to have come all the way from Quincy. So,
BJ quietly followed her in the night and waited her out to see
what she was doing.*

BJ was the only one who saw her there that night.

And Daisy was grateful to him.

He kept his mouth shut.

A pair of headlights stole Daisy's attention as a white '23
Jeep Wagoneer Series II pulled up into the entrance of the

BP gas station. Recognizing BJ's truck, she then stepped out of the shadows alongside the store.

Daisy hurried over to the truck and snatched the passenger door open at once.

"You a'ight, Dai?" BJ asked the second she slid into the seat and shut the door. She shook her head no, and BJ nodded seriously, putting the truck in gear and swerving back in traffic.

"Me and Von are at odds right now."

"Why?" he asked.

Daisy opened her mouth to answer, then the ringing of her phone prevented her from doing so. She reached into her pants pocket for her phone. When she looked at the screen, Daisy was surprised to see that it was Twan's number calling her.

She answered. "Hello?"

"You got some explain' to do, Daisy."

She sighed. "I know, Twan."

"I spoke wit' Rikah already. She already don' laced me up. But I still wanna hear your side of thangs. Which means we need to meet up," he said.

"I'm still here in town."

"I know," he replied.

She paused. "All you gotta do is say where, and I'll be there," said Daisy.

***

Dawn had come, and soon the night would turn to day, and there would be no ore hiding in the shadows. But Lank didn't care one way or the other, as he worked the two wires beneath the steering wheel of the Cadillac DTS to manipulate its start of the engine. Next to him, waiting in the other car, was Lil Earl, who was anxiously telling him to hurry up. They were stealing a car right from the lot of a local used car dealership in the Gretna area.

About twenty minutes ago, during a traffic stop on Second Street, Lil Earl was forced to make a concrete decision. By this time, cops were pulling everybody over, and they had witnessed at least seven traffic stops along the way. The authorities were searching for anybody and everybody that slightly even looked like they were street dudes. Chief Moore wanted to make a firm statement in the streets and had assembled a three-unit task force and went out to shake down everybody they knew to be street dudes and take them all in whether they were guilty or not. And Lil Earl and Lank knew this and were not going to chance trying to talk their way out of anything. So, as soon as the cop got out of his patrol cruiser and was about a foot away from Lil Earl's door, Lil Earl stomped on the gas pedal and jetted the car through a maze of side streets and back roads to evade the police.

Lank thought it best to head into the Gretna area where they were far away from the inner sections of Quincy. They had gotten away and were proceeding to switch vehicles for safety purposes.

It took Lank a minute to start the car, and when he did, Lil Earl wasted no time hopping in on the passenger side.

"Took your ass long enough," Lil Earl said smartly, as he relit his Black & Mild.

"Shut the hell up, Lil E!" Lank killed the lights until he was back into traffic. He pulled out and put the Cadillac about fifteen yards away from the car they came in with. Lil Earl then took up the Mac-11 and protruded it out the window at the other car. He aimed the gun at the car's gas tank area and let it loose.

The sixteenth shot was what did it, and the car blew the fuck up right there in the lot. And Lank got the hell out of dodge, knowing the explosion had alerted all types of people.

Meanwhile, Lil Earl was pulling out his phone and scrolling through the social media channels to see what the latest news was. The last thing he heard was that the cops were snatching niggas up left and right throughout the town. Word had traveled through social media for all the hustlas and goons alike to be careful out there, but Lank and Lil Earl already knew this. They were careful, but the cops were too amped up on vengeance, so nobody was safe.

Which was why Lank asked Lil Earl to duck lower in his seat because his dreadlocks were evidence in itself and a reason for the cops to pull them over again. So, Lil Earl laid low in his seat, and they rode in silence, as their thoughts took their own course.

Once they were back in town, Lank drove the speed limit. By this time, the sun was rising over the horizon, and daylight was bringing everything into view. And just as they had witnessed before, people were getting pulled over all over the place. The police cruiser that was in pursuit of them earlier could be anywhere by now, and Lank could only hope that they never encountered another one on this mission.

Lank found himself back in Pepper Hill, on Key Street, where Cody and Alisha lived. Following his first mind, Lank drove along the street in hopes of catching his man. To keep from dozing off like he felt himself doing, Lil Earl went about exchanging clips in the Mac-11 since Rontay had had an extra three fully loaded.

"Ohhh." Lil Earl looked up and said after seeing where Lank had taken them.

As the car neared both homes, Lank watched as another car pulled out into the street in front of them from a neighboring driveway. He slowed the Cadillac to allow the other vehicle to situate itself. Moments later, they were back in motion and were just passing Ms. Donna's house when Lil Earl spotted someone entering through the front door of Cody's house.

"I saw it," Lank replied when Lil Earl gestured up ahead in the direction of the house in question.

Lil Earl said, "Let's crush 'em, brah. Right now. Let's get our lick back!" He had unlocked the safety on the Mac-11 and sat anxiously in his seat, as they drove right past the two houses slowly.

Lank, although quiet, wasn't going to miss out on this opportunity. For all he knew, that was Cody who had walked through the front door of his house. He only caught the movement at its last second. If he was going to take this chance, then he wanted it to be done right. No way should Cody escape from this fate.

Time for payback.

Chapter 8

The person Lank and Lil Earl were mistaking for Cody was actually Bebop. He had to go check on Menace next door like he was told to do by the others. Menace was still in Alisha's bed knocked out cold, so Bebop wrote him off as being okay. Then, he went back over to Cody's house where he left the game he was playing on Cody's new XBOX on pause. Bebop couldn't wait to get back to kicking ass on *Grand Theft Auto*.

Back inside the living room, he set his gun next to him on the sofa. Bebop reclaimed the wireless XBOX controller and resumed his play.

Before leaving him by himself to hold the fort down, Cody told him how important it was to remain brave and discreet. He warned Bebop about the dangers of his and the others' adversaries, saying that he should not allow nothing or no one besides family to come near him. No one could be trusted. To shoot first and ask questions later. Bebop assured Cody that he could do it, that he was up for the task he'd set out for him.

Bebop was no stranger to danger. He'd flirted with danger most of his twelve years of living. Being the son of a strung-out addict would bring danger around when you weren't looking for it.

He had to grow up hard. He was tough.

Bebop had his own secrets, his own skeletons in the closet, some that he was afraid to admit to anyone for fear of being treated differently.

Like what happened to him two years ago. The night he was caught behind Burger King, dumpster diving for scraps of food the employees would trash out back at closing time. Apparently, he was trampling on someone else's mission and was caught slacking between the back of the metal dumpster and the concrete bricked cove structure that hugged its space. That night, Bebop was beaten up and sodomized by a grown ass man and left behind the dumpster, bleeding from his rectum and in severe pain.

Bebop would never forget that horrific moment in his life when he literally thought he was about to die.

Then, two weeks later, Bebop ambushed that very same man with Hell-Boi, who was a vicious, full-blooded red nose pit bull that belonged to Tony Dred from around the corner. Bebop and Hell-Boi laid in wait for him behind that same dumpster. When he stepped inside that space, Hell-Boi attacked. For several minutes, Bebop watched as the dog ripped into his enemy and heard him scream. But Bebop was far from done with him. He called Hell-Boi off, and then he doused the man with a jug of gasoline. Two blocks away, you could hear the petrifying screams bellow from the burning man as Bebop and Hell-Boi fled the scene. And even then, Bebop was still hurting in his backside from the damage his enemy had caused him.

So, when Cody made him give him his word that he would handle his business, Bebop did so with a confidence that couldn't be denied.

And then, he saw it — the shadow of somebody moving past the window outside. Bebop knew this for sure because the entertainment center where the XBOX was connected to the TV set directly in front of the living room window. So, when Bebop saw the shadow of someone walk by the window, he became instantly alert and grabbed the gun beside him.

Tossing the game controller aside, Bebop shot up to his feet and dashed for the hallway.

Right then, the back door exploded inwardly, and to Bebop's surprise, it was Lil Earl, and the menacing look on his face only said one thing.

Kill.

Bebop upped his gun and let off one shot in Lil Earl's direction, as he was spinning on his heels to rush the other way. But then, the front door was kicked in, and Lank barged inside with his pistol ready. Instinctively, Bebop shot him twice in the chest area, dropping him! Then, a hail of automatic rounds sprayed from Lil Earl's Mac-11 behind him as he pursued him.

Next door, Menace was immediately awakened by the sound of gunshots. With a groan, he reached for the Glock near his good hand and pulled himself out of the bed. Then, he made his way out the room and toward the sound of war erupting.

In the process, Bebop was darting out of the front door. Another round of bullets sprayed behind him, and suddenly, Bebop was pitched forward by one of the slugs punching him in the back. The impact sent him airborne and flying off the porch and landing hard on his face in the dirt.

Lil Earl gazed down at Lank, as he laid dead in the living room doorway. He shook his head sadly and then proceeded to go finish Bebop off for good. By now, he was all in. Lil Earl was committed and being discreet about it was out of the question.

Crying out in excruciating pain, Bebop glanced behind him and saw Lil Earl stepping out the front door. He then began to crawl away by using his arms because, for some reason, his legs couldn't move. Every move he made was an explosion of pain and agony.

As if he had no reason to hurry, Lil Earl descending the porch step made him look even more wicked, as he glared down at Bebop with this approach. But all that changed when, suddenly, Menace called out his name from next door. Lil Earl turned his gaze in that direction, and Menace began dumping hollow point rounds at him, as he came hurrying across the front lawns. Lil Earl ducked and ran back through the front door of the house.

Meanwhile, Bebop was slowly fading away, as he watched Menace take chase after Lil Earl. But there was no catching him in the condition he was in. Menace could barely move with his body being weighed down by exhaustion and a heavy dose of medication and grief. But that gangsta in him refused to allow anything to keep him from doing his duty.

A menace to society.

And Bebop was bleeding to death.

Little brah was down.

***

Another cigarette break was just what Tami needed, and she asked Felicia to come outside with her. The only ones left inside with Teddy were his mother and Marolyn. Everybody else left to go home and wherever their life courses took them. Tami was tired, and she needed her rest. Shequita had already told her several times that she needed to either go home and get some rest or find one of the vacant rooms in the hospital to find rest. Everybody was tired and exhausted from the emotional strain, and it wouldn't be long before their bodies suddenly shut down. And when that happened, there was no getting back up.

Outside, Tami shook out a cigarette and passed the pack over to Felicia. They lit up and stood there quietly for a minute. The sun was slowly sneaking its presence back over the eastern horizon. Another day was being born, and there was no telling what it would bring upon their lives.

"I've been thinkin', Tam," said Felicia, as they stood off from the hospital's entrance doors.

"About what?"

Felicia exhaled. "Been thinkin' about takin' that job offer down in Orlando wit' my cuzzin', Tanya."

"Smart move."

"But you know I don't wanna leave…"

Tami stopped her with a lifted hand and said, "Leavin' Quincy is the best thang you can ever do for not only yourself but Av and Ava. All this mess we goin' through right now should solidify that decision. Go, gurl, and don't let nothin' stop you. I love you, and I want to see you safe and happy for a change."

A brief silence passed between them. Felicia looked out into the traffic along the main highway. "I don't have no home anymore," she said.

"Stop that." Tami turned a frown on her.

"I don't, Tam."

"Felicia, home is wherever the heart is, and what's mines is yours. Quincy will always be your home. But there comes a time where happiness in your own home ain't present, and you need to go build anotha one. Give yourself a fresh start down in Orlando. Hell, maybe you'll finally find yourself a damn man for a goddamn change." Tami smoothed a little tease in there to lighten the mood a little.

"What about you though? After all this, what you gon' do?" she asked.

"You know I ain't never leavin' this damn town, gurl," said Tami. "I'm stuck here."

"Never say never." Felicia nudged her with an elbow.

"I'ma die right here in Quincy, sista."

Her friend's choice of words made her uncomfortable. It made Felicia want to hug Tami but knew any affection was the last thing she wanted right now.

"So, Cody and Ray?"

"What about 'em?"

"What's your take on that? I mean, you think Cody gon' just accept that shit for what it is? You know how headstrong he could be at times," Felicia said and took a quick pull form her Newport. "But after what happened wit' Wes and Corey last night, Ray coming into his life at this stage might be too much for him."

"Too much of what?" Tami asked.

"Pain. Betrayal. Confusion. You know he's gonna hate you for all that shit?" Felicia turned her attention fully on her friend to gauge her reaction. Tami was good at carrying her pain. She kept a real poker face, so much so that Felicia couldn't tell whether her words really struck a chord or not.

The entrance door opened, and Officer Amanda Turner and Faye exited the building. Manda's face was swollen badly and clearly bruised black and blue, as a thick white bandage covered her nose in what appeared to be a makeshift splint of somewhat. The woman looked like she had gotten her ass beat up and was wearing it proudly.

But it was Faye Bradwell that awarded Felicia's attention the most. Her and Faye used to be archenemies back in the day. But over the years, they had put their childish beef aside and conducted themselves like adults. Though it was Tami who didn't care too much about the older woman next to Manda, and it had nothing to do with the fact of her being a cop. Tami thought Manda was genuinely cool and likewise. They even once shared a bottle of wine together some time back.

Here were four women with different objectives who were obviously affected by the latest atrocities.

Faye was the first to make a move and headed in the other women's direction.

Tami braced herself for a confrontation.

"How is Rontay doing?" Felicia replied the instant the two women came to rest before them.

"By the grace of God, he made it through," said Faye, a tall, slim built woman in her mid-forties whose dark complexion shone under the morning sky.

"What about you, Manda?" Tami directed her attention on Manda, who stood there looking pitiful.

"I'm alright," she managed.

"What happened?"

"The same thang that happened to all of us," Faye interjected. "I lost my son last night. Y'all lost people you loved too. Family going against family." When she said this, she glanced over at Manda, and Tami caught that look and wondered what that was all about. "We need to come together somehow, someway, and put an end to all this mess round here."

"It's too late for that," said Tami.

"It's never too late, Tami."

"What can we possibly do after all the blood that's been shed out there?" said Felicia.

"I mean, what can we even do?" When Manda said this, she captured all their attention. She was a cop, and it was clear by her words of expression that she was all out of options. At least those where intervening wouldn't cause them any further pain or loss in the process.

"Something has to be done," said Faye. "There's gotta be something we can do."

"When you figure it out, Faye, lemme know," Tami said before flicking away her cigarette. Then, she turned around and walked away from the group.

"Felicia?" Faye said pleadingly.

"It's too far gone, Faye. We already did what all we could. It has to balance itself out in its own way. Okay?" she replied.

And then, Felicia took her leave.

What else was there to say that would make any sense whatsoever?

It was war.

It wouldn't be over till it was over.

Chapter 9

Patricia "Pooh" Howard was brewing her fresh pot of coffee when there was a knock at her front door. She backed out of the kitchen, as her ears tuned in to what was being broadcasted over the morning news station coming from her stereo sound system. Pooh headed for the front door, peered out through the peephole, and hurriedly unlocked the door.

"Well, good morning to you too, niecey!" Pooh said animatedly, as Von brushed past her into the house without so much as a hello.

"Hey, Pooh." Remmy stopped to peck her on the cheek before following Von inside. Pooh shut the door and locked it behind her, as she stared after her sister's daughter and her sidekick.

"Where's Daisy?" Pooh also knew this was Von's most trusted sidekick of them all. Let her tell it, Von and Daisy were no different from the other. They were both designed to be tight due to their capabilities.

At the mention of Daisy, Von shot her dear auntie a stern look in return.

"What's ailing you this early in the mornin'? The last time you paid me a visit this early, you had the police after you," said Pooh.

Von stopped pacing the living room floor. She gazed up at her auntie, and Pooh would have sworn she saw the devil in her eyes.

"Is the police lookin' for you, niecey?"

"No," Von lied.

"Then what's going on? C'mon. I got some fresh coffee in the kitchen. We can talk all about it in the kitchen." Pooh didn't wait and made her way into the kitchen without further ado.

"She knows all my moves but one, Remmy," Von said before she began pacing the floor again.

"What's that one?" he asked.

Von told him that she couldn't disclose that notion to anyone. It was one of those things that she vowed to hold close to the chest.

"And you sure she doesn't know?"

"I'm very careful when it comes down to that, Remmy. Not even God knows about this one." That meant that Von was the sole person with the knowledge of whatever this was that she claimed to have held so strongly a secret that no one knew.

"God knows everything we do," said Pooh.

Von turned to face her. Pooh was standing in the kitchen doorway.

Remmy's phone rang, and he got up to go take it outside out of Pooh's earshot. Apparently, the woman was good at eavesdropping on shit.

"What is it that you're not tellin' me, Vontoria?" When Pooh spoke her full name, Von knew that her auntie had run her patience thin. "You gotta tell me somethin'. You barge into my house pacing a hole in my carpet and with blood on your clothes, not to mention with a gun on your person. You know how I hate those thangs, Vontoria. You look scared and dangerous all at the same time. It's scaring me, niecey. Please tell me what's going on with you," said Pooh, a devoted ninth grade language arts teacher and a damn stubborn woman when she wanted to be. Seeing the sudden fire in her auntie's eyes, Von knew she would either have to tell her something or turn away and walk back out that front door.

The last thing Von wanted was to expose Pooh to any more danger. It was dangerous just having her as a niece. But in her heart of hearts, Von knew Daisy wouldn't dare hurt Pooh. That killer in her just wouldn't let her do it. Not to Pooh Baby as Daisy called her.

But then again, it wasn't really Daisy she was worried about where her auntie's well-being was concerned.

It was Rikah and her vicious antics, and Von knew her heartlessness was something to stress over.

Those killas could be on their way right now to Midway to target her beloved auntie.

"You're in danger, Aunt Pooh," Von finally said and brushed past her again to enter the kitchen this time.

But before she could get far, Pooh reached out and grabbed ahold of her arm.

"How am I in danger?" she asked.

Right at that moment, the bathroom door opened down the hallway, and a half naked man with a towel wrapped around his waist appeared in the kitchen doorway. Von looked up and instinctively drew her Beretta and aimed it at the stranger who now stood before her.

"No! Niecey, stop!" Pooh panicked.

The stranger, a much younger man than one would have thought Pooh would be seen around with, looked at the gun and tossed his arms up in the air. He stood there with a red toothbrush in his mouth and eyes big as saucers with fear.

"Harold. Please leave now!" Pooh approached the man and shoved him back down the hall where they then entered the master bedroom.

The front door opened, and Remmy entered and made his way toward the kitchen. When he entered, he looked at Von and then at the gun lying on top of the kitchen counter.

"What's the word?" asked Von, undecided on whether she should pour herself a cup of coffee or a glass of cognac from the door of the fridge.

"That was Dutch," he said.

"Okay,' she waited for more.

"I laced him up on everything and told him to get the crew ready and wait on my call."

Von nodded. "Good. We just might need your little goon squad to assist us now."

Remmy was proud of the team of young killas he had recruited. They were separate from the group that he strengthened with Von and Daisy. His young and ruthless seven-man crew were called the STB Gang, which stood for Secure The Bag, which also meant that they were about that money bag — no matter what it took to get it. Dutch was the chief enforcer and also Remmy's little cousin who he held dear.

But it was the second from the last youngest of them all that Von was crazy about. His name was Yellow, and she was just wild about him.

He was more hers than he was Remmy's. But overall, Yellow was loyal and true to his mission.

Von decided on a cup of coffee, as she filled Remmy in on what just took place before he walked back in the house.

"Pooh got a man?" He seemed surprised by this.

"Obviously." Von shrugged with nonchalance, as she sipped her Folgers coffee carefully.

"Then that must be his Charger parked out front in the driveway." Remmy didn't care for coffee and opened the fridge to snatch one of Pooh's cans of Sprite soda she had inside.

Moments later, the bedroom door opened, as Pooh escorted the man to the door and out of the house. In passing, Von caught a glimpse of the nigga, and he glanced at her with a troubled look on his face.

"Sorry about that," said Pooh a minute later after seeing her companion out.

"Who the hell was that, Auntie?"

Pooh sighed and said his name was Harold, and he was another schoolteacher at the school where she worked.

"He looked young as hell too," said Remmy.

"Vontoria?" Pooh turned her attention to her niece. "Now, what is this mess you're talkin' about me being in danger? Why?"

"You obviously didn't hear about what happened to Daddy yesterday," said Von.

Pooh shook her head. "I heard about the kid attackin' him, but what does that have to do with me, niecey? Help me understand that concept," she said. Then, she took up the coffee mug that she had already prepared for herself before being distracted.

Von told her what her aunt needed to know, including the part about Daisy's betrayal and the possibility of her coming there to do her harm.

"No," Pooh was shaking her head wearily, "I don't believe she would do anything to hurt me."

"Which means you don't know Daisy like you think you do, Pooh," Remmy replied, and the look he got back in return was one of pure fear.

"I'm calling the police," said Pooh.

"And what the fuck would that do besides watch 'em fuck up like they always do?"

"Then," Pooh stepped up into Von's face and glared into her cold, hard eyes, "you better go out there and do what you do. Because I can assure you this, Vontoria," she inched a bit closer to the point their noses were almost touching, "if anythang happens to my big sista, I'm coming for you my damn self. Do I make myself clear?"

"Aunt Pooh," Von replied.

"What?"

"You better back the fuck up off me," she warned.

***

The meeting spot was back at Money Mel's crib, and when Daisy and BJ pulled up, they found Cody standing outside the house waiting.

76

The call from Twan was just to establish contact with her after speaking with Rikah. But then he wanted Cody and the others to link with Daisy and possibly come up with a master plan to win this war. Meanwhile, Twan and his crew were linking up with Rikah and her people and strategizing from that angle.

Cody stared out after the white truck as it came to a halt at the curb. Behind him, Avery and Money Mel were inside the house going over some things that needed going over. Po'Boy was sitting out on the front step with his gun in his lap and was watching the coming and goings all around them.

The doors of the truck opened, and both occupants got out. At the sight of BJ, Po'Boy grabbed his gun and rose up to his feet to face them head-on.

"Easy,Po'Boy," Cody said to him.

"I'm easy," he muttered.

Daisy led the way toward the house like she was on a mission. The closer she got, the clearer it became to Cody who she was. It felt strange having her show up now after knowing that she had been siding with the enemy beforehand.

Cody could care less about the nigga she was with, but he figured Po'Boy was already locked in on him anyway. Cody wanted to hear her out. He needed Daisy to give him one good reason for him not to put a bullet through her face too.

"What's up, Cody?" she greeted him humbly.

"Sup," he stood firm.

Daisy then introduced BJ as her friend and a solid nigga who was there to support her. BJ needed to be spoken for because his presence spoke volumes of its own. It was clear he was a man who seemed like he was actually about that life.

"Where you from, homeboy?" Po'Boy asked, refusing to just take Daisy's word for it.

"Havana," he said. "Rich Boy."

"Rich Boy, huh? You know Monte Herring?"

"That's my little podna. Why?"

Po'Boy nodded and whipped out his phone to make a quick call.

"He's definitely official," said Daisy.

"Maybe in your book he is," Cody replied and held her gaze intensely. Daisy looked at him and instantly recognized that glint in his eyes. She knew a killer when she saw one, and there was no denying the young one that now stood before her.

What bothered Daisy most was that it took her all the way up until now to realize this factor. She would never have guessed him to be.

When Po'Boy confirmed BJ's status, Daisy smirked and said she told him so. He shrugged and let them both inside where the others were.

Inside stood Avery in just a bulletproof vest, cargo shorts, and sneakers, while Money Mel lounged on the sofa, inspecting his selection of arsenal. Everything was laid out before him on the table. Upon Daisy and BJ's entry, he took up a Wilson Combat 1911 .45 caliber and sat back in his seat humbly.

"Hello, Melvin," greeted Daisy and carried herself over to where he sat and laid into the seat beside him. BJ remained standing but only at her side while he looked around the room attentively.

Po'Boy informed Avery and Money Mel on who BJ was, and Money Mel only nodded in answer.

"So, what's going on? Why you switchin' lanes from your girl, Von?" asked Money Mel.

Daisy didn't hold anything back, as she spoke her peace. To hear that she had recognized him in the video that had gone viral made Cody intrigued. Then, she went on to explain her actions from the moment she realized Cody was her cousin up until that very moment.

Avery dropped his head at the mention of Von killing Ty. He was angry about it. Avery felt cheated somehow. Ty was supposed to be his man.

"One less nigga we gotta deal with," said BJ, seeing the look on Avery's face.

"Von and Remmy is the major problem right now."

"It's not just her and him," said Daisy.

Her words caused Cody to look at her through slitted eyes of silent alertness.

"There's this crew of younstas that Remmy has recruited that could be a major problem for us. It's no doubt in my mind Von knows I've made contact wit' you guys now. Which will be all the reason for her to utilize the STB Gang to get her numbers up," added Daisy.

"STB Gang?" Avery shifted uneasily.

She nodded. "Plus, Von is wealthy enough to employ further souljas if she feels the need to."

Po'Boy was also utilizing his phone to communicate with Rod in regard to the things Daisy was sharing with them at that moment.

"But Rikah is doing her part too?" said Money Mel.

"Good thang we got Twan 'em out there in Tallahassee right now," said Cody. "They're supposed to meet up wit' Rikah and her people."

"Which is a good thang like you said, cuz. Rikah and her man pretty much run Tallahassee, and they got major influence in the streets there. Cuz got her own army, and this Von knows, which would encourage Von to do the unthinkable to get the advantage."

"The unthinkable like what?" asked BJ.

Daisy shared with them a few things Von was capable of doing when her back was against the wall. Von was a whole other monster when pressured.

The room was silent for a moment, as thoughts of Von's unthinkable capabilities left them all wondering.

"By now, Von has prolly made it back to Tallahassee to regroup," said Money Mel.

"Where she's more comfortable on her own territory," said Po'Boy, looking up from his phone. "Despite the threat she knows Rikah and her people to be, plus all the shit you know about her, Von is smart enough to use that as a tool to stay ten steps ahead."

That was when Money Mel got up and stepped over to the minbar to pour himself a shot of scotch. Something was worrying him about this whole situation. With all the odds stacked against Von, it was her caliber and distinguished survival antics that made all that shit seem so useless somehow.

The bitch was smart.

She was thorough

"But there's one thang I know that Von doesn't think I know that we prolly can use against her," Daisy said.

"What's that?" asked Cody.

Reluctantly, Daisy said, "Her little son."

"Son?" Money Mel spun around to face her. "Von doesn't got no damn kid," he replied.

"That's the point," she answered. "That's exactly what she wants you to believe."

Chapter 10

The Impala SS turned sharply onto Shade Farm Road, and as Ray directed his course onward, the blurb of a police siren responded behind him. Ray peered into the rearview mirror and cussed under his breath, irritated that a cop was actually pulling him over when they apparently knew who he was. Ray angled the car along the curb. *If there wasn't one thing, it's another*, thought Ray, as he sat there in frustration, wondering if he should get out or remain behind the wheel. Behind him one white cop he knew as Fred Brewer and the Black cop, Lynn McKinney, both got out and approached his car. The expressions on their faces were stern, as it appeared obvious they didn't want to be there.

From his rearview mirror, Ray watched as Officer Lynn McKinney reached up and switched off her body cam. It was then that Ray expected some type of seriousness was about to transpire.

"Ray." Fred was the first to speak up.

"What is this, Brewer? You pulled me over while I'm on my way to a crime scene?" said Ray Williams.

"Please step outta the car, Ray."

"Why?"

"Step out. Now!" Lynn demanded while resting her hand on the handle of her sidearm. "Don't make me tell you again, Sarge," she hissed threateningly.

Grudgingly, Ray shook his head and opened the car door and got out. That was when Officer Lynn McKinney grabbed ahold of him and shoved Ray roughly against the side of the

Impala SS. Brewer then stepped up and clasped the cuffs on his wrists.

"What the hell is this all about?" Ray replied. A second later, he felt a hard jab into his kidney by Lynn and a vicious growl at her partner.

"You got my friend killed, Ray," said Lynn. When Brewer placed his wide frame on the left of Ray, that was when Lynn began punching him hard in the ribs with her fist. And this wasn't a little lady for Lynn was known around the department for being a hard ass.

Police brutality was the norm in certain situations, but Ray never expected that he would become a victim of it himself.

Vehicles drove by along the street, and the two cops would pretend as if they were conducting themselves professionally. But when the coast was clear, Ray was assaulted further by Officer Lynn McKinney. With every blow to the ribs and kidney, it reminded Ray of why he was being targeted the way he was.

Both Lynn and Detective Sharon Eddison had come in through the academy together. The two were very close friends, and now that Sharon was dead, Lynn intended on making Ray feel her wrath.

"Don't know what the hell you got going on out there, Ray, but you're giving yourself a bad rep in the house," said Fred, referring to the Quincy police department.

"I'm doing my fuckin' job!" Ray snapped.

Lynn snuck a short jab to his jaw and said, "Your job? Four dead, Ray! Four! Your job is to fuckin' detect!" She kneed him in the side and pulled out her Glock. "You worthless piece of shit, I should kill you myself and do us all a goddamn favor."

"Lynn," Fred said with earnest.

Turning Ray around to face her head-on, Officer Lynn McKinney had tears in her eyes, as she glared up at him. "Sharon was like a sista to me, Ray."

"You think I don't know that?" he retorted.

"Shut the fuck up!"

Ray hushed.

Lynn sneered, "You don't wanna know what Chad and Leo want to do to you right now."

At the mention of Sharon's husband and her state trooper nephew, Ray could just imagine what they were going through right now. Ray felt like the piece of shit that Lynn said he was.

"You got twenty-four hours startin' from right now to find Sharon's killer. Or so help me God, I'm gonna put a bullet in your ass next. And I swear that on Sharon's grave, muthafucker!" Officer Lynn Mckinney no longer wanted to share the same air with Ray and headed back to the waiting cruiser.

Brewer uncuffed him and just shook his head, not bothering to say anything to Ray. He made his way back over to his police car and drove away. As they passed, Ray watched as Lynn aimed an imaginary gun at him and pulled the trigger. *Boom.*

One shot was all it took.

It did with Sharon.

Now Ray was really mad. He got into the car and sped away. His body ached from Lynn's assault. That was her whole intention — a reminder of what was to become of him next if he fucked up again.

Ray thought about the chief and the confrontation he had with him before and after Sharon's murder. Then the relentless fear Rayneshia showed toward him. Then the vow from his wife, Latrice, that she was going to stay with her sister and for him not to show his face. Latrice was tired of him and all the bullshit that surrounded him. The deaths of Sharon and Ty and the other two boys was the nail in the coffin for him. What he had shared with Latrice was dead now. A separation was now in effect.

Everything was going to shits for him.

It made him want to cry.

But Ray knew he had to turn up now. Everything was on the line. He had to find Von and kill her. But most of all, Remmy was to be terminated like the fuckin' roach he was.

Ray knew it was Remmy who had killed Sharon that morning. He was not saying that Von wasn't capable of doing it herself. But Remmy was a different kind of killer from the rest of his street associates. His file read like a Mitch Rapp bad guy in one of those David Baldacci novels. The nigga was not only just a street dude. Remmy did two years in the U.S. Army before being dishonorably discharged for smoking weed and selling guns, which landed him in prison for five years. Prison only made him worse. Remmy got out and made a name for himself as a hitman for hire while selling heroin on the side. Then, he linked up with the likes of Daisy and Von, and since then, his street rep had elevated to something more prolific.

Remmy was a stickler for weaponry and was quite versatile with his killing methods.

He was raw.

But Remmy was also slippery. He always found a way to slip through the cracks. Questioned for over fifteen murders and not one indictment.

So, he had to go just as well as Von, and Ray was not going to do it by law. It was time that he put his badge aside and got down and dirty with this shit. If they wanted his attention, then they damn well had it now.

His destination was Key Street where another murder scene took place. When he got the call from Detective Franklyn Grant to stop by, Ray feared the worst had come. He prayed it wasn't Cody whose body was found dead in his house.

When he got there, the whole area was crawling with people. Here it was, another tragedy on Key Street and at Tami's house at that! Ray had no doubt Tami would pack up and move away after this ordeal.

"They got Lank this time, Ray," said Frank, who had been waiting at the curb outside the house when the Impala pulled up and Ray got out.

"Damn," muttered Ray. "What happened?"

That was when Detective Aliya Bush approached with a hard look on her face. She was fairly new to the force, having transferred from Tallahassee a little over a year ago. Her Aunt Ruthie Mae got sick, and she was the more dedicatedly reliable person to look after her.

"Aliya knows more than I do, Sarge." Frank gestured toward the female detective.

Detective Bush gave them the full rundown on what went down, including Bebop being airlifted to be delivered to TMH to undergo immediate surgery.

"No," Ray couldn't believe his ears "Not little Bebop," he whispered in weariness.

"We also believe the shooter was Lil Earl," said Frank, frowning. "But nobody's naming names."

"Not even the one who came to Bebop's rescue," added Aliya.

"The neighborhood's protectin' their own," said Ray knowingly. "Why wouldn't they?" he dwelled.

***

Who would have believed an actual kidnapping was being done right under the noses of those occupying the ICU ward of the Tallahassee Memorial Hospital? It went to prove that during the act of war, nothing was to be underestimated.

When the door to the hospital room opened, Dez looked up at Jazz's entry. Jazz was dressed in nurse scrubs and a face mask and eyeglasses to disguise her identity.

"Where's brah?" asked Dez, who was Jazz's older sister by two years. Both were beautiful and of the mulatto complexion. But it was Dez who was the more ruthless of the two, while Jazz had the brains, not saying that Dez wasn't intelligent as well.

"He's preparing the car for us to leave," said Jazz from behind her mask.

The person they were speaking of was Malik, the third wheel and the actual muscle to their crew.

At the side, hidden away from the door, was Sonya Roberts and Reyzyne, both Von's most beloved people to whom she would give her all. Both women were hogtied and gagged. Scared and helpless.

It all happened from one simple act of manipulation of the mind. Reyzyne and Sonya decided to take a break from being cooped up in the miserably suffocating room watching over Vince. They had only just stepped out to go purchase a few things from the vending machine around the corner. It was then that Jazz approached both women and convinced them that the removal of Vincent Roberts to another room was in progress at that very moment.

"What room is he being moved to?" asked Reyzyne, petite and soft pecan brown skin with bowlegs.

"I'll show you," said Jazz. "Follow me."

And that was how they were led into the room where Dez immediately took charge. She ordered both women down on their faces on the floor at gunpoint. They complied, and together, both sisters bound the two women. Then, they waited for Rikah's call to set the bait in motion.

Von didn't bite, and her actions weren't effective enough for Rikah.

The next order of business was to have the two women abducted from the hospital to another location where Rikah could be more hands-on.

The tricky part was getting them away without alerting anybody that any foul play was amiss.

That was when Jazz left and came back with two wheelchairs, two face masks and comforters, and a couple of hospital gowns.

"Let's get to work then," said Dez once the plan was laid out to her.

Within ten minutes, they had Reyzyne and Mrs. Roberts dressed in gowns and face masks and perched into both wheelchairs. To anyone other than themselves, the two women looked like hospital patients.

Jazz looked over at her sister and told her to text Malik to let him know they were coming.

"A'ight." Dez pulled out her phone.

And that was when Jazz took up her gun and bashed both women alongside their heads to knock them out. Now they sat slumped in their chairs.

"Ready?" said Jazz after covering them with the comforters.

Dez nodded. "Always ready."

And just like that, the two sisters wheeled the women all the way out the hospital into the waiting minivan that Malik had stolen.

No words were spoken until they were in traffic, and it was Dez who spoke up.

"I don't know why she don't just let us off these two hoes," Dez said after removing her own face mask, revealing a bottom row of diamond encrusted gold teeth.

"I guess she got somethin' else in mind," said Malik.

"I wonder what." Dez fired up a blunt.

In the back, Jazz was rechecking the two women's bound wrists. They were both still unconscious and had no clue of the fate that was coming to them.

Malik said, "Where we going anyway?"

"The dungeon."

"Oh," Malik muttered. At the thought of the dungeon, it reminded him of the last time he was there. Things had gotten really messy then.

The dungeon was located on Crawfordville Highway at an old residence that beheld one of the few underground basements you could find in the city. The dungeon was down in the basement of the house, and it was owned by a trustworthy associate of Rikah's.

The drive took them about twenty minutes to make, and when the minivan arrived at the location and Dez saw who it was that accompanied Rikah and their crew members, she all but bolted from the moving vehicle.

"Oh, shit," muttered Jazz.

"What?" Malik replied curiously as he watched.

Jazz said, "There goes Twan."

"Who is he?"

That was when Jazz frowned at Dez after she opened the door and literally jumped out the minivan before it got a chance to park. "The only nigga that can ever turn my sista into puddy on sight."

Chapter 11

"You know what? Fuck that. I ain't duckin' them muthafuckas," said Von over the roof of the car at Remmy. "Let's spin the bend on them niggas one more time before we head back out."

"Back in Quincy you mean?"

She nodded.

Her and Remmy had just spent the last thirty minutes strategizing on warfare and how to utilize the little leverage that they still had.

Fearlessness and stealth and influence.

Now there she was, wanting to return back to Quincy and possibly land them in a suicidal situation. But Remmy was not bitching about it. He lived for that gutter shit.

They headed back to Quincy.

Meanwhile, Pooh was headed off to work at East Gadsden High School. Before parting ways, Von pointed out to her that she wasn't exempt from being another casualty of war. So, she provided Pooh with a fully loaded Walther P22 pistol to keep her safe.

"I don't need no damn gun," Pooh told her. Growing up with three older brothers, Pooh was accustomed to using her hands to settle differences.

"You will when them goons pull up," said Von.

"Goons?" She gave Von an odd look.

As she headed back to Quincy, Von wondered if her auntie really had it in her to pull the trigger when it was time. Before leaving, they reached a mutual understanding that Von hoped Pooh would honor.

"I know Daisy prolly thinks I've gone back to the city by now," said Von.

He lit a cigarette to smoke. "She knows you better than most people do."

"Only what I want her to know, Remmy."

"You said that too."

"But I want my little boo right now though. I don't know why I even left him behind to miss all this fun." Von pulled out her phone.

Yellow. Remmy had no doubt she was referring to his young protégé. It always left him feeling a little jealous inside when Von got all endearing over Yellow. There it was, he was killin', hanging out, and vying for her attention and praise on a more personal level, and all he got was a head nod or some dap. Rammy was far from ungrateful. All he wanted was for Von to acknowledge him sometimes at least in the same fashion as she did Yellow.

Why couldn't he be her boo?

Why did he have to compete with his own protégé?

"Hold up, Yellow. I got the hospital callin'," said Von, as the incoming call came through. She then switched over and answered. "Hello?"

"It's me, home girl," the voice said.

Chloe. Von shifted in her seat. "Talk to me, Chloe. What's going on?"

"Reyzyne and your mama is gone. The doctor went in this morning to check up on Vince, and nobody was there. I thought maybe they stepped out for a second to get some air, but it's been a whole hour now. Ms. Sonya woulda never left him for that long without somebody reliable lookin' out for him," said Chloe with conviction.

This Von knew, and it awakened something in her heart to also know that her mother and Reyzyne were probably dead by now.

"Just keep your eyes open, home girl."

"You know I am, Von."

"But my daddy is a'ight though?"

"He's good," she said. "Doc just got done doing some more tests on his eyes."

"But he's still in a coma?" said Von.

"Yeah," murmured Chloe.

With a shake of her head, Von disconnected with her and switched back over to Yellow. It gave her mind a sense of gratitude to see that Yellow was patient enough to wait for her to switch back over. That said a lot about his character. Yellow had the patience of a killer.

"I want you and Lil Herb here in Quincy asap," she said to him. "The rest of the team are to touch everythang Rikah and Daisy own and love. No exceptions, boo." Von was seething, furious.

Remmy was surprised that Von tossed him the phone, and he retrieved it while Yellow was still on the other end. Out of the corner of his eye, he saw Von close her eyes and lean her head against the window.

Von felt like something was taking hold of her heart and squeezing the life out of it.

When she said what she said earlier when Rikah contacted her, Von spoke out of fear. Or was it really coldness? All she knew was that it wasn't her time to go yet, and she was not going to sacrifice herself. Why when her loved ones were going to die anyway? May as well take the loss and use it as fuel to execute vengeance on the enemy.

Kill them all in the worst way.

And shit on their graves.

After conducting his talk with Yellow, Remmy hung up with him and turned his gaze back on Von. "There's only one place they coulda taken them, Vee."

"I know," she said.

The dungeon. It would be the only place where the likes of the mother and wifey of one of the most treacherous bitches in the streets would be taken and disposed of. It was just three and a half months ago when Remmy and Von were both there conducting murder business. The dungeon was accessible to only a select few.

"But Rikah knows this too and prolly thinks I'm stupid enough to go there."

"And walk straight into her trap," said Remmy.

Von said, "I ain't that stupid."

***

Teddy was wide awake when Tami came into the room, crying, and Marolyn was then startled awake from her sleep. Marolyn asked her what was wrong, and that was when Tami told her about Bebop.

"Bebop? Who is Bebop?" asked Marolyn, looking up at the other woman who had followed Tami into the room. "And who are you?"

"I'm Kim," Daisy's mother replied smartly.

But suddenly, all attention swept over to the bed where Teddy exploded in a rage. He began snatching the IV needle from his arm, doing away with the tubes, and shoving the bed covers off of him.

"Teddy, no! Stop. Stay in the bed!" Tami panicked.

"Where my clothes?!" Teddy demanded, as he tried to get out of bed before Tami rushed over and got in his way. "Gotta go check on Bebop."

"No," she said.

"No?" Teddy sneered up at her. He thought about it for a moment, took a deep breath, then reached out and shoved her away from him. "My brotha needs someone! Gotta go to him," he said.

Both Kim and Marolyn looked at one another in silent dismay toward the situation.

At two hundred fifteen pounds, Teddy was no easy feat to restrain when he was determined to have his way. He got out of bed on unsteady legs but quickly righted himself to move productively. Looking around for his clothes to put on, Tami shrugged and told him the fresh set of clothes were stored in the storage compartment underneath the bed.

"Get them for me, Mama Tee," he said.

Tami didn't even hesitate.

"Where's Quita?" Marolyn asked.

Shequita had headed back to the house with Felicia to grab a few things she needed. She said that she wouldn't be long, but with Teddy up now and raising hell, it would be good if Shequita sped up the process of whatever she was doing. Because from the looks of things, Teddy wanted out, and Lord knows what he was capable of doing next.

After Tami handed him his clothes and shoes, Teddy went into the bathroom to change into them.

That was Kim's cue to call Shequita and tell her what was going on.

The door opened, and Brandi entered the room with Latrice in tow. Instantly, Tami went from zero to one hundred as she rushed Brandi like a fullback and collided right into her.

"Ohmigod!" Marolyn went into a panic.

Tami was all over Brandi like flies on shit, kicking and punching and cussing up a storm. Brandi actually tried to fight back, but Tami had more control by the grip of her $100 weave. And she was wearing her ass out like she stole something.

"So, y'all just gon' stand there?" asked Latrice.

Without further ado, Kim moved forward to break up the beatdown Brandi was receiving. Then, Marolyn and Latrice joined in with their assistance.

"Bitch! I should kill yo' black ass!" Tami raved from beyond Kim and Marolyn's shoulders as they forced her back to the other side of the room.

"What did she do?" Marolyn wanted to know after Brandi picked herself up and hurried out of the room, holding her bloody face.

"That was her man," said Tami, breathing fire.

"Her man? What man are you talkin' about?" Kim was asking with puzzlement in her expression.

Tami said, "The nigga they found dead in my house this mornin'. That was that bitch's man. And he prolly the one that shot my baby boy."

She was referring to Bebop.

"Cody?" Latrice gasped.

"I woulda killed her ass off top." Tami leaned back into the wall and stared down at her hands. They were bloody and bruised. Kim rested her hand on her shoulder and offered a word of comfort to her.

A momentary silence ensued.

It was then that Tami finally looked at Latrice and realized she was actually in her presence. Tami came off the wall with a start.

"Yes, Tami, it's me," said Latrice humbly.

"What are you doing here, Latrice?" Tami moved toward the detective's wife, and Kim laid a hand on her arm to keep her at bay.

"I came to see you and offer moral support," Latrice replied with direct eye contact.

"See me? About what?"

"To let you know that I know the truth about Cody being Ray's son. And that I forgive you, Tami. I truly do," said Latrice.

For a moment, Tami was speechless. She had always wondered how the moment would be when her and Latrice finally came face to face if the truth ever came out. In her mind, it was violence and a lot of cuss words. But apparently, everything didn't happen the way one expected it to.

"Will you accept my blessings, Tami?"

Kim leaned on her friend. "She will accept, sista."

Reluctantly, Tami nodded her head.

"Um, where is Teddy?" said Marolyn.

This was cause for Tami to break away from them and hurry across the room. She looked in the bathroom, and no one was there.

"Shit!" Tami rushed for the door, opened it, and stepped out into the busy hallway. She then ran toward the exit route at the front of the hospital, and Teddy was nowhere to be found.

Marolyn came hurrying after her with a disturbing look on her face. "Tami."

"What?" Tami sized her up, troubled.

"It's gone too," she said.

"What's gone?"

That was when the woman leaned toward Tami and whispered to her. "He took the gun too."

Instant dread swept through Tami at the thought of what Teddy had just done.

Shequita was about to lose her mind.

Her baby was gone.

Chapter 12

When he was fleeing from Menace's blazing gun, Lil Earl wished he would have gotten away unscathed, but he didn't. Unfortunately, one of the bullets had grazed his head just above his right eyebrow, and the wound was bleeding like crazy. Lil Earl had to literally get away by using one eye because the heavy blood flow from his wound prevented him from seeing out of his right eye.

Lil Earl panicked when he thought the bullet was lodged in his skull. This scared him so bad that he took out his phone and called for immediate medical attention.

He called Ms. Fix It.

He called Sand because the last thing he wanted was to show up at the hospital.

After telling Sand where he could meet her, Lil Earl swiftly and stealthily maneuvered his way through the Pepper Hill territory. He had damn near been spotted by a roving cop several times who was seen by some passersby who just regarded him offendedly, but yet no one dared to hinder his mission.

Sand was waiting patiently for him out front of the Sunset gas station on High Bridge Road. He had made it all the way there from Key Street to the gas station behind Carter Paramore's school football field. He saw her work Jeep and hurried over to get inside in the back.

By this time, Lil Earl had taken off his shirt and had it pressed against his head. Blood was soaking through the balled-up shirt, and the heavy loss of blood was causing him to become dizzy headed.

"Just keep pressure on it, Earl. I'll be right to it in just a little while," said Sand, as she sped out of the station's exit.

"Don't tell nobody I'm wit' you right now either," Lil Earl warned her.

"C'mon, Earl. I respect the code. I take my job very seriously, and you outta all people should know that," said Sand straightforwardly.

He knew that to be quite true. About a year ago, Lil Earl was shot twice in the leg and the stomach during a carjacking mission. He had been caught lacking outside a new bitch's crib that he met on the Gram when two young niggas ran down on him with those thangs. Lil Earl was in his money green Lexus coupe and called himself bucking the jack on those young niggas and got toasted.

Good thing Sand wasn't too far from the area and showed up right on time. "Yeah," he managed. "I know whatchu mean."

"Oh, you better, nigga!" Sand pulled up into her parking garage twelve minutes later and helped Lil Earl into the gated residence of her five-bedroom home that she'd renovated into her workplace. Her loyal assistant was awaiting their arrival and already had a room set up for them to work in.

Lil Earl was laid out on a surgical operation table and given something liquid to drink for his pain. Then, his body relaxed, and before he even knew what was happening, Lil Earl slipped into a deep unconscious state and remained there.

"Like a baby," remarked Sand. When she said this, there was a dark, sinister look to her hazel brown eyes that spoke a story of their own.

Then, she left the room quietly.

The next time the door opened was fifteen minutes later, and Cody entered the room followed by his brothas, Avery and Money Mel. They came in and shut the door behind them so that no one else witnessed what was about to happen.

When Lil Earl phoned Sand earlier, she then called to inform Twan. Twan notified Money Mel, and that was how they came by sharing the same room with Lil Earl.

Hours ago, prior to Trey's murder, Twan had called and shared some names with Sand of who she needed to watch out for in case of an emergency. And Lil Earl's was one of those names. Sand's loyalty was to the nigga who promised her her heart's desires and h*onored* that promise.

So why not keep it real?

At the sight of Lil Earl lying on the table, Cody thought back on the last time they were face to face.

Then came the resounding words in his head of what Menace said he stopped Lil Earl from doing. He had already shot Bebop and was about to finish him off for good.

Bebop would have been dead.

"All because of you, nigga." Cody didn't realize he had spoken out loud until it happened, and Avery responded to his words.

"And now you gotta die," said Avery.

With the quietness of an approaching storm, Money Mel stepped forward and slapped fire from Lil Earl's face. He stirred on the table. Another vicious slap brought a groan out of him. But it was the third one that sent his eyes fluttering open.

Cody snarled down at him like a wild hyena when Lil Earl finally registered who they were. Then, he produced the jack iron in his hand for Lil Earl to see. Beside him on the other side of the table, Lil Earl looked over at Avery, who was clutching a hammer.

"Please…" Lil Earl began to beg, but Money Mel stopped him with a punch to the mouth.

Then, Money Mel took a few steps back.

And then, Cody and Avery went in for the kill. The first blow from the hammer shattered Lil Earl's left cheekbone on impact. He screamed, and Cody went across his right jaw with the jack iron, breaking it instantly. Then together, they proceeded to beat Lil Earl to death right there on the operation table.

Looking on silently, Money Mel was reminded of Zed's death the night before by Twan on that pool table. That was some vicious shit, but what he was witnessing now was pure animalistic.

This one was gruesome to a higher degree.

It wasn't long before Lil Earl's face was completely caved inward from the brutal weapons. Blood was splashing everywhere. He was dead already, and yet they still continued to beat him.

They beat him for Bebop.

For vengeance.

But most importantly, for the hunger of that beast that was patiently waiting to be fed again.

***

Rayneshia was sitting behind the wheel of her car, texting on her phone, when a Crown Royal purple colored BMW M2 pulled up on the scene. When she laid eyes on the shiny car, Rayneshia felt her heart skip a beat. Then, she opened the door and got out of her car and was approaching the BMW when she spotted Teddy exiting through the side entrance of the hospital.

"Teddy?"

He paused and looked up at her through wary eyes and a battle wounded face.

Rayneshia then rushed over toward him, and Teddy drew his gun at once. That brought her to a halt immediately.

Seeing that he'd made his point without verbally speaking it, Teddy proceeded his trek across the crowded parking lot of the Quincy Hospital. In his other hand, he carried a Hyundai key device to which he repeatedly pressed its button to activate the car's security soundcheck. He kept pressing it until he located the right car and got in.

"The fuck is going on wit' that nigga?" said Qay, who was now standing outside his purple BMW with curiosity written over his face.

Rayneshia spun toward his voice and hurried over to where he stood. "That's Teddy, bae."

"And who is he supposed to be?" he asked.

"He's my little brotha's best friend."

"What little brotha, Rayneshia?"

Several yards away, Teddy was backing out of the parking space and enroute to the main highway. That was all Rayneshia needed to see to jump into the BMW and yell for Qay to get in the car.

Qay got in indeed, but he didn't dare move until Rayneshia explained herself first.

"Just follow that car, bae. Please!"

"For what?" said Qay. The next look Rayneshia gave him was evidence enough to make him pursue the car that Teddy was getting away in.

A minute later, Teddy turned toward town, and Qay soon made the turn behind him.

In the process, Rayneshia shared with her man everything that'd happened since they last saw each other. She also uploaded the viral video of Teddy's attack at the rec center. It was then that Qay remembered actually seeing the video once before.

"So, you actually have a brotha?" he asked.

She nodded. "I met Cody for the very first time a few hours ago, bae. It wasn't what I expected, but we got a good understandin' now."

"You make it sound like there was an issue."

"It was pretty rough, bae."

"What did he do?" Qay turned his gaze on her and looked her over. And that was when he noticed the bruises along her neck. Suddenly, his eyes clouded over with fury. "That nigga put his hands on you?!" he spat venom with his words.

"Calm down, bae."

"Naw. Fuck that. No nigga gon' put his hands on you like that. Brotha or not. Little brah gotta see me, bae. Real shit!" he snapped.

What Rayneshia really wanted to tell Qay was that he'd be barking up the wrong tree. Cody would kill him. Or his brothas would. So, it was best that she made him understand this clearly before he found himself in a bad situation.

Rayneshia loved herself some Qay McGriff. His thuggish ways and that protectiveness toward her made her feel secure. Qay was street royalty, a thoroughbred go-getter, and he also had integrity about himself. But right now, he was feeling crossed, and that would make him quite deadly as well.

In the two years Rayneshia had been committed to Qay, she could count on one hand the times she'd actually witnessed him harm another human being. Qay tried not to bring his street affairs into their relationship, but that street shit was just embedded in him.

He was a certified goon.

Thuggin' was his way of life.

The streets raised him.

"So, what we followin' him for? He obviously don't know who you is. What's your plan?"

Rayneshia didn't have a plan. Then it hit her. She had to let Cody know what was going on.

"Now you fixin' to call this nigga," Qay said when he saw her dialing on her phone.

"Shush, Qay!" Rayneshia reached over and rubbed his chest soothingly. "This is the plan, bae."

He just shook his head irritably.

He thought he was finally being summoned over to spend a day with his girl and her family, but it turned out he was headed slap right into a warzone.

It was Money Mel's number that Rayneshia was given to get in contact with her brother. He answered on the second ring, and it was Avery who answered.

"This Rayneshia, Av. We got a serious problem."

"Teddy?" he said knowingly.

Her heart swelled. "Yeah. I'm followin' him as we speak."

"Where you at?"

She told him.

"Don't lose him," said Avery. "We'll catch up in a minute."

Up ahead, Teddy turned left down the side road between the Old Sacks grocery and the pharmacy building. It was right there on that little narrow street that the Hyundai Ioniq came to a sudden halt.

Qay had just turned onto the same path and entered the parking space area when Teddy suddenly hopped out of the car. Both Qay and Rayneshia watched as Teddy lifted the gun and began busting shots at their car. Rayneshia screamed in horror, as the car they were in shook from the multiple rounds slamming into it. Qay instinctively grabbed his bae and shoved her down, as the windshield spider webbed across the front of the car. But just as swiftly as it happened, it ended with Teddy hopping back in the car and racing away from the scene.

When all was quiet, Qay lifted up his head and peeked over the dashboard to check the view.

Teddy was gone.

"You okay, bae? Lemme see you." Qay helped Rayneshia sit up and saw that she was badly shaken.

"I… I'm alright." Rayneshia stammered over her words and shuddered in aftershock. Qay looked over her body, checking for wounds and found none.

Outside the car, people were coming out of the buildings and observing the scene. One older, Black guy in a fishing cap came over to the car and stopped outside Qay's window.

He asked if they were okay, and for obvious reasons, Qay could not answer him.

"You know we can't stay like this, Qay. We gotta go. We need to get away from here," said Rayneshia, slowly subsiding from her tremendous scare.

Still Qay didn't say a word. There was a dark look in his eyes. He stared at his ruined car, his pride and joy, and a murderous quake awakened inside of him.

"Bae?" She stared at him.

Without a word, Qay left off the brakes and allowed the BMW to proceed forward. They moved through the little street and turned right onto the next street over.

"I'm sorry, Qay," cried Rayneshia.

No reply.

The only talking he wanted to do was to let his pistol speak for him.

No words could express his feelings.

Only gunplay.

And Teddy had just made himself another enemy.

Chapter 13

Dez watched with quiet curiosity as Twan took the call he'd received and stepped out of the room to conduct the call privately. She had just made it back up from the basement after preparing a message to Von by chopping off her mother's left hand with a machete. It was also recorded, and there were even photos of the gruesome scene it created. Rikah was very much aware of the psychological mind games Von liked to play. So, every hour, a piece of her loved ones would be delivered to her until that shell securing her cold heart cracked open. This was Rikah's form of playing mind games. And Dez took pleasure in doing the blood work.

Twan and Rod and Souljah were also present in the room when Dez did her thing. But Twan just shook his head in disdain and separated himself from the wickedness he'd witnessed.

Dez assumed that he no longer wanted to be around her in that setting, that the beautiful, intelligent woman that he had a habit of reminding her that she was to him was not living up to the light he put her in.

Did he hate what I did? she thought. Was she pushing him away with her lifestyle?

Before he left, Twan had stared Dez directly in her eyes and shook his head. Where she thought she was impressing him with her ruthlessness, Twan did not like it the whole time. That shit affected her. Dez wanted to go after him and demand to know what he thought of her now. She wished for him to call her beautiful and tease her like he always did when they got together.

What had she done?

Twan was not being the Twan she knew.

He seemed different.

Of all the hardcore street gangsters she knew, Dez would say that Twan was at the top of her list. It was more so because his gangster was genuine — or it was at one point — but something was totally wrong now.

Dez was in love with the nigga. Simple. And now he was switching up on her, playing on her emotions. Shit like that was a very dangerous thing.

Tossing caution aside, Dez stepped out the back door of the dungeon just when Twan was ending his call. He looked up at her with a solemn expression. But he didn't say anything, and that made her a little uneasy.

"Are you a'ight, Twan?" Dez hated herself for how soft he made her when she tried so hard to keep her cool. "Are we okay?" she asked.

That seemed to have somehow pulled him out of the fog he was in a moment ago.

"That was my godmotha," said Twan slowly. "My sista was killed yesterday evening, and my godmotha needs me to be there when she makes the funeral arrangements."

"But you don't have the strength to do it."

He shook his head no.

"I'm sorry, Twan," she expressed.

"It's not your fault so don't apologize."

Dez ached for him. The urge to hold him in her arms was powerful, but she resisted that urge for fear of making him more uncomfortable.

What she really wanted was for him to fuck her brains out. To pound her goon-style and break his dick off in her guts. Anything to relieve him of the stress. He needed it. He needed a real bitch to hold him down.

"How did she die, if you don't mind me asking?"

"It's already been handled, Deziree."

A surprised look crossed her face at his words. One look in his eyes told the meaning of what laid behind that statement. Twan's sister had been murdered, and her death was avenged.

That was what made her do it. Dez stepped forward and pulled Twan into her arms. At first, Twan's hard body tensed up from the sudden act of affection. Then, beyond his own control, his body relaxed, and he hugged her back. Dez squeezed him tighter, and no words were needed.

She was his comfort.

This was her gangsta for real.

The moment only lasted briefly before Souljah exited the house along with Rikah. Both of them were astounded by what they were seeing, Rikah especially because she knew how crazy Dez was over the nigga and how Twan never showed any affection whatsoever for anybody except for his sister.

"I changed my mind," said Rikah.

"About what?" asked Twan.

Rikah, who was jet black but pretty as a kiss and more dangerous than a cage full of rattlesnakes, met Twan's eyes intensely and said, "I'm killin' them two bitches instead and hittin' Von's ass where it'll hurt worse."

"What brought on the change, Rik?"

"Daisy."

"Daisy? How?" Twan regarded her, puzzled.

"She just called me and provided us wit' a whole other angle that we can tackle. It may take a trip to Jacksonville to get it done though."

"What's in Jacksonville?" asked Dez. She purposefully stood herself shoulder to shoulder with Twan and brushed her arm against his to let him know she had his side.

Twan gave her a quiet, knowing look.

"His name is Shyleek Branch, and he's two years old, and he's the ultimate, most important piece on the board."

"And why's that, Rikah?"

"Because he's Vontoria Roberts' son," said Rikah with that devilish glaze in her eyes. "And I want him. And I want to make his mama suffer. Badly."

"Didn't know Von had a son," Twan replied.

Right then, Dez began snapping her fingers repeatedly with that look of someone trying to remember something when it was right there on the tip of their tongue.

"That time in the indoor flea market on the southside when that old nigga, Durk, got his throat cut. When Von got ghost for about a year behind that shit. If I'm not mistaken, the timing of two years old sounds about right. Damn. That slick bitch!" said Dez.

The back door opened, and Savage stepped outside amongst them. These was Rikah's top enforcers: Dez, Savage, Beanz, and Boobie, but it was Savage that she favored the most, and it had nothing to do with him being her man's brother. This nigga was so official that once, even the Black Mafia Family wanted to recruit him.

"Who is slick?" Savage wanted to know.

Twan told him who.

"Oh, yeah," Savage replied. "She's slicker than a can of oil."

He lit a cigarette as Rod and Souldjah let themselves out while the cleanup crew took care of business inside.

"I know a coupla people over in Duval who owe me a few favors. I can set it up, but I'ma need more intel on the little one," said Twan.

Together, Rikah and Twan broke off from the group to speak more privately. When Dez moved with him, Twan gave her that look without ever speaking on the matter. She remained humble and pulled out her phone.

Rikah led him over to where her teal green colored Maserati MC20 Cielo sat parked out back near the minivan that needed to be disposed of quickly.

"What's up?" Twan ran a hand absentmindedly over the Maserati's smooth body.

"I didn't wanna bring it up around the others, but I know you're hurtin' right now, and I'm sorry about Lisha. That was my gurl," said Rikah. "But there's something you might not know about Lisha, and I think you should know this, big brotha."

"You wanna tell me some personal shit that you know about my sista now that she's dead. It was the reason I didn't know in the first place when she was alive. So, no, I don't wanna hear it, Rikah. Before she died, Lisha was happy, and even in death, I want that to still remain in my consciousness. Her being happy. Nothin'…"

Rikah cut in. "Alisha was happy, and she will always be, but that doesn't change the fact that she was living a double life, Twan."

"A what? A double life?" He stared at her and noticed something hidden beyond her eyes.

"Yes. Your sista was a happily married woman to a great man and their little boy."

"What?!"

Rikah nodded. "Now do you wanna hear?"

***

Ray was driving along the neighborhood street when, suddenly, he noticed Shequita's car parked in her driveway. When he'd last seen it, it was parked at the hospital, which meant Shequita had finally come home for a little break.

Before Ray could talk himself out of it, he swerved the Impala in along the curb out front. At that same moment, a gray Hyundai came charging up the street. It then nosed into a stop two feet from touching Ray's car.

"The fuck is he doing…" Ray muttered in surprise after recognizing Teddy behind the wheel.

Teddy then climbed out the car. His face was all screwed up, and he looked quite menacing. Ray damn near broke his neck getting out of his car.

"Teddy?" he called out.

At the same time, Teddy looked his way but kept right on pushing toward the front door of the house. Then, the front door opened, and Felicia rushed out to him. Ray watched them exchange words briefly, then Shequita appeared in the doorway, and that sent Teddy resuming his mission for the house. Shequita let her son through, but then she stared out at Ray with open interest.

"He escaped somehow?"

"Apparently," she said. "Come in if you gon' come in, but I got to go check on my son." Shequita held the door for him, and Ray slid in past her.

"Any idea how he managed to get away? I'm sure that you left him in the care of your people."

Shequita said, "There was a situation at the hospital, and he slipped out unnoticed. Tami called and told me."

"And what situation was that?"

Teddy called out to his mother, and she turned away from Ray for her son's bedroom. She went inside and shut the door, and Ray was left alone in the living room.

From beyond the bedroom door, Ray could hear the agitation in the voices of Teddy and his mother. Then, a thought came to mind, and he pulled out his cell phone. Something had to give, and he knew just the person who could provide him with what he needed.

Ray stepped outside on the front porch to take his call. "I need a favor from you, Bumpy."

"The fuck you callin' my phone for, nigga?" came an aggressive voice which belonged to Bumpy Gilyard, the cousin of his wife, Latrice, and a retired gangster who still kept ties to the streets. He and Ray never did get along because they had two agendas, different beliefs, and plus Bumpy was once on his radar in connection to a couple of murders.

"My back is against the wall right now, Bumpy."

"What the fuck that gotta do wit' me?"

"Latrice," he said.

A long pause.

"So, I get to finally kill you for hurtin' my cousin now, huh? It took you long enough," Bumpy said.

Staring straight ahead, Ray watched as two cars drove past the house and bypassed a known crackhead he knew by Clara. "No," he answered. "It's not about that. But there's somebody who's potentially aiming to do that."

"Who?"

"Her name is Von Roberts."

Bumpy seemed to dwell on this factor. "You must really got a death wish, Ray. Now how did you go and get crossed up with that young, crazy gurl?"

Bumpy obviously knew who Von was, and it didn't surprise Ray one bit. She'd been raising hell in the streets for years, and her reputation was without flaw.

Ray told him.

"She's one of Dot Brown's protégés," said Bumpy. "Before Dot crossed her and then Dot got murdered."

This surprised Ray. "I didn't know that," he replied, having been reminded of the late female gangster who had a passion for taking in young female strays and teaching them the game. "I thought Dot had a heart attack?"

"She did."

"Then, how is it that Von killed her?"

"Because," said Bumpy, "you can only imagine the terror Von took her through to put so much fear in her heart that her heart burst from it."

When the body of Dot Brown was found in her home, she still had the look of petrifying terror on her face. It was as though she had literally met the presence of pure evil. Like Freddie Kruger came to life. Dot's death was viewed as suspicious, but nothing more came out of it.

Ray wondered how he knew so much about Von, but he decided against asking him.

"So, Von is threatening you and has put my cousin and her daughter in harm's way." Bumpy paused for a second to consider his next words. "As you should know, Ray, that is punishable by death in my book."

"I agree," he said.

A purple BMW came rolling up the street toward the house and came to a sudden halt next to the Hyundai in the middle of the street. When Ray looked toward the car, there were two things he noticed instantly. The windshield was spiderweb cracked with a bullet hole emphasizing its obvious torment. And there was a fog of steam spewing from beneath the hood of the BMW.

"Oh, shit!" Ray replied when he suddenly locked eyes with Rayneshia sitting in the passenger seat.

"What is it, Ray?" said Bumpy.

That was when the driver door opened, and Qay jumped out immediately. In his hand was a chrome pistol. Ray saw this and reacted quickly.

Qay was moving around the car just as Rayneshia got out and hurried toward him.

Marching in their direction, Ray watched as his daughter reached for the guy, and he snatched away from her. Then, he stepped over to peer into the window of the Hyundai. Then, he glared in the direction of the house.

"No, Qay," said Rayneshia. "Let's just go!" She reached for him again, but Qay was immovable.

"Rayneshia?" Ray arrived upon them. "What is going on? Who is this guy?"

Rayneshia ignored her father and gave the other guy her undivided attention. Qay sneered and upped the pistol as if to shoot rounds at the house before them.

"Qay, no! Please," she pleaded with him.

"Tell that pussy boy to bring his ass outside…" Qay said, and then another car came charging in their direction. When he turned to look, he didn't waver nor shy away the pistol in his hand.

But then the car screeched to a halt before the BMW, and all four doors opened at once.

Rayneshia swallowed nervously when Cody, Avery, Money Mel, and Po'Boy jumped from the car. Every last one of them were strapped with artillery. And all it took was for Qay to breathe wrong and they were going to light his whole world up like it was Christmas time.

Chapter 14

For about ten minutes now, Von and Remmy had been parked in the hospital parking lot. She didn't like going against her own word, but this mission was cause for greater measures.

A moment ago, Von received the photos of her mother and her wifey's horrible deaths. She couldn't lie. It hurt like hell. All that tough shit was gone out the window. And the silent tears that streamed down her face at that second was from the anger that boiled inside her. The murderous rage was burning like hot lava in her.

Now that she knew her mother and Reyzyne were dead, Von no longer cared about another soul.

Vengeance cracked her sanity.

The beast within her was banging against the walls of her brain. She was contemplating going up in the building and killing everything that moved. She wanted to kill children and all. Everybody. Anything to satisfy the hunger of the beast dwelling within her.

And that hunger intensified when Tami, Marolyn, and Latrice Williams exited from the hospital's entrance. When Von laid eyes on the three women, she sat upright in her seat. She zeroed in on Latrice as a dark sneer crossed her face. Von knew this was the detective's wife and also the mother of her enemy's best friend. The third woman she had no clue of, but Von didn't care. They all were about to die.

The women approached a brownish colored sedan as Latrice peered inside and then scanned the parking lot area.

113

She opened the door and reached inside for what appeared to be a cell phone.

"I'ma take care of this one," said Von.

Remmy just nodded quietly. He knew how badly Von wanted to create havoc right now. He could literally feel the rage vibrating from her side of the car.

The car the three women were standing outside of was parked about twenty yards away. The expression on all three women was one of puzzlement and worry.

"There goes Yellow," said Remmy, gesturing toward the main highway as a black and red Cadillac Escalade truck with dark tinted windows turned into the entrance of the hospital.

Von wasn't hearing him nor interested in anything but the three women in her line of vision. Sometime during the wait, Von had materialized with Remmy's butterfly knife.

She flipped out the six-inch blade and growled at her own reflection in the stainless-steel weapon.

Von opened the door and got out. The big Cadillac truck was edging closer, as Von eased around her vehicle in the direction of the three women. She placed her hands behind her back in a nonthreatening manner like some people did.

Across the parking lot, Tami and the other two women got into the car. Von was several feet away from going in for the kill, but them getting inside the car complicated her mission.

Then again, it didn't because she could still make a move. She could still utilize this opportunity to gain leverage on the situation.

And that was exactly what she did. Von rushed forward just as the car was pulling out of the parking space. She snatched the rear passenger door open and slid into the backseat. Then, in that same stealthy fashion, Von snaked her arm around the driver seat and placed the blade of her knife against Latrice's throat.

The car jerked to a stop instantly.

Next to Von in the backseat was Marolyn, who cringed in fear of the woman with the knife. Tami turned a pair of glaring eyes back at her.

"Say it," Von dared her with an even gaze. "Say somethin' fly and I'll slit her fuckin' throat right here."

Not that far away, Yellow and his homie, Turk, turned onto the path leading to the car loaded with women. But the truck came to a stop behind the vehicle that Remmy was occupying.

"What you do to her ass won't affect me, little gurl. I don't know who you think I am," said Tami, not seeing the fearful look Marolyn was presenting.

Von hissed and said, "Then have it your way." She ran the blade across Latrice's neck and then drew her gun in the same breath.

But not before Tami drew hers first. At the same time, she aimed it at Von's face and pulled the trigger. Instinctively, Von moved her head just as the bullet would have slammed into her right eye, but instead, it dug a deep graze along the base of Von's skull. The gun in her hand let off two rounds, which missed Tami by inches in the close area.

Before Von could even say stop, Tami was already bolting from the car.

"Arrggh!" Von roared after her, as she reached a hand up toward the burning sensation of her wound. One moment, she saw Tami, and the next second, she was jetting past the rear passenger door.

Von shot after her from inside the backseat of the car. Sitting next to her, Marolyn was so petrified that she forced herself down onto the floor. All Von saw was the back of the woman's head.

"You too, bitch!" Von aimed and sent four slugs, punching Marolyn in the back of the head and neck.

More shots rang out outside the car, and when Von looked up, she saw Tami taking aim at Yellow and the others. Then,

Tami took off running around the corner of the building out of sight.

She had underestimated Tami and had damn near gotten killed in the process.

Out of the corner of her eye, a shadow passed over Von, as she got out of the car. It was Yellow and Turk who had come to her rescue.

"C'mon, Vee. We hot right here... You hit?!" Yellow gasped when he looked at Von and saw her bleeding from her head. "Oh, shit! You hit!" He panicked and circled an arm around her protectively and guided her hurriedly toward their truck.

"Oh, no. Remmy." Von immediately became saddened when she saw Remmy lying on the pavement. It didn't take a rocket scientist to know that he was dead.

Yellow forced her to bypass Remmy's corpse, as he pushed her into the rear entrance of the Cadillac Escalade. He shut the door and rode shotgun, as Turk gunned the truck's engine toward the Highway 90 route.

"Who was that bitch?" Turk demanded.

Von gritted her teeth furiously.

"That bitch murdered my nigga," said Yellow. He was humble, but the murder in his eyes shone like a lightbulb.

Von pulled her shirt over her head, fighting back the pain in her head, unaffected by sitting before her crew in a sports bra. "We ain't heading back. We stay down here."

"Huh?" Yellow turned to face her.

She looked at him. "I want that bitch's head," Von said, pressing her wound with the balled up shirt. "And I ain't leaving till I get it."

"Say no more." Yellow nodded seriously.

But little did they know of the heat that was about to fall upon them this day.

Von's doomsday. Her game was almost over.

All things must come to an end.

***

BJ and Daisy had taken the back route entrance of the hospital just as Von was headed back toward town. It wasn't until they found a parking space on the shoulder of the brick structure around the corner and got out did they hear the alarm. Both of them looked at one another, and Daisy stepped over toward the corner of the building and gasped.

"Daisy! Cuz?!" Daisy heard the familiar voice and turned in its direction.

It was Tami standing in the side door entrance of the small hospital. When Daisy saw her mother, Kim, standing just behind her, her heart squeezed with panic.

Daisy rushed toward them.

"What happened around there?" she asked.

"Von," was all Kim said.

The name caused Daisy to frown, as her mother and Tami filled her in on the situation. Next to her, BJ eased Daisy's hand into his and squeezed it reassuringly, letting her know he was still there.

"You shot her?" asked Daisy, and Tami nodded her head gravely. "Damn."

"I tried to kill her ass." Tami then told her about killing Remmy and about his other enforcers.

"Yellow." Daisy knew automatically when she described him.

"Who is he?"

"One of Remmy's guys, Turk too. But Yellow is Von's favorite, and wit' them being together right now after what transpired, thangs are about to get even more crazier," said Daisy.

Tami asked her younger cousin to take her away from there, and Daisy did not leave her waiting. They all piled into BJ's ride and got away from the scene before the wrong people spotted Tami.

117

In the process, Daisy shared with Tami all she had gone through since they last saw each other.

Kim shook her head miserably, as she listened to Daisy talk. To hear that Latrice lost her life today brought on a cold shiver that ran through her. And Marolyn, who she herself had taken a kind liking to the woman, her death made her feel so damn bad.

"Take me home," said Kim.

"No," Daisy objected. She was not about to risk doing that, and Von knew about it. At this stage, Von was at her highest degree of murderousness and killing Kim would be a great pleasure.

At this point, Von was beyond caring.

Suicidal.

That was when Daisy went on to share the plan they had for Von.

"Vontoria has a little child?" Kim replied and shot her daughter a weary glance.

"Take me to Jacksonville right now," Tami replied.

"Hell no!" Daisy blurted out.

"I'm not fuckin' asking you," said Tami. "I'm tellin' you to, Daisy. And you will show me where he's at."

BJ interjected to tell Daisy that he had been meaning to tell her about that matter. "My brotha, Shawn, and his people live out there in Duval," he said.

"I got Rikah on it as we speak," said Daisy.

"But I'd already contacted brah, and he's on the move right now as we speak," he added.

"You shouldn't have done that, BJ," she said.

"Why not?"

"Because," Daisy replied, "it will interfere in what Rikah got going on. You know how particular she is about thangs like that, BJ."

BJ let out a heavy sigh and reached for his cell phone.

In the backseat, Tami said, "I don't give a fuck. I want that little bastard myself…"

"Tami," Kim gazed in her direction, "let them do whateva they do. You've done enough already."

"Fuck that," Tami shrugged. She thought about Bebop, and she knew she needed to be there for him. No one was there at his side, and Tami asked BJ to just take her there instead.

Fifteen minutes later, Kim was dropped off in the Old Projects where her godbrother, Dino, lived. Dino was a well-respected man in the OP, and its territory was well-guarded. One couldn't just come in there and raise hell and expect not to be punished for their actions. This was the third most dangerous place in town.

Back on the road again, headed for TMH, the conversation led back to Von and her acts of war.

"I thought she had gone back to Tallahassee by now," said Daisy.

"Well, you thought wrong, cuz." Tami lit her last cigarette and stretched out along the backseat. Suddenly, her thoughts went to Ray, and Tami pulled out her phone to call and tell him about Latrice. Then, she refrained from doing so because she knew it would hurt him. She didn't want to hurt the man who was out there battling the cold streets to save her son.

"It's already done," said BJ after reading the text message he'd just received.

"What's already done, BJ?"

"They got the boy."

"Who?" Daisy knew it was a dumb question the instant it left her mouth. Then, she sucked her teeth and said, "Now here comes the bullshit."

Chapter 15

Teddy was standing over the bathroom sink, staring at his hideous reflection in the mirror. He had removed all the bandages and only his swollen, stitched up face was presented, a sight that seemed to awaken a dark hatred in Teddy, and he wanted to deliver the same cruel treatment to somebody else.

Somebody had to pay for this.

Anything to relieve himself of the rage that consumed him like a tub full of sulfur acid.

There was a knock at the door, and Felicia called through the door to him. "Your brothas are outside," she told him.

That was all Teddy needed to hear. He reached for the door and stepped out into the hallway. Teddy was shirtless. The wounds along his upper torso and back area were just as profound. Tink Tink had really done a number on him, and he would never forget that.

Teddy had some very serious plans for her next. The girl he once loved would feel his wrath.

Without saying a word, Teddy marched down the hall toward the front. He bypassed his mother standing out on the doorstep. When Teddy saw his brothas, he swelled with pride, but when he laid eyes on Rayneshia, something in him switched off. Then, he spotted the same purple car he'd shot up earlier, and that beast in him smelled blood in the air.

Teddy registered something serious was amiss and headed in the direction of his brothas.

"What's up?" Teddy muscled himself into the circle of his brothas to come face to face with Qay.

120

"I see you didn't want no trouble, Teddy. It's all my fault. I told him to follow you," said Rayneshia.

Teddy sneered at her. "The fuck you followin' me for, bitch?" he snapped, and Ray flinched at the disrespectful remark toward his daughter.

"She's my sista, brah," Cody replied grudgingly, glaring in Ray's direction. Then, he turned fully around to face Teddy with a further explanation on the situation.

Now, Teddy was glaring up at Ray and moved over to stand before the man. His wounded, flabby chest rose up and down in growing outrage. Ray gave the boy a side eye, and that was when Teddy punched him hard in the gut and sent him doubling over in pain.

"You might be my brotha's daddy, but you don't get no respect from me," said Teddy before looking back over at Qay, "and you can die right now, or you can join the team, nigga."

"We join," Rayneshia spoke for the both of them and didn't dare look her father's way.

"Let the man speak for himself, Rayneshia," said Po'Boy, who was at Qay's left with his Glock out and ready to make it bang.

"Yeah," said Cody. "So, what's it gon' be, nigga? You gon' ride or slide?"

Qay glared at them all, obviously unafraid but cautious and smart enough to keep his personal comments to himself. Then, he said, "I didn't come down here for all this shit. And now that it involves my girl, damn right I'm down to ride. But there's a condition to that." He turned his attention fully on Teddy. "You put me and my girl in danger when you shot my car up."

"He did what?" Ray blurted out.

Teddy just shrugged.

"So, when you get healed, just know I'm coming for that fade, lil' nigga!" Qay told him.

Money Mel stepped up right then. "You don't have to wait for that," he replied. "Fade me."

"Nah, Mel, I got this," said Avery while pulling off his shirt and handing his gun over to Cody.

Ray's cell phone started ringing, and he answered it as fast as he could.

"Right here," Avery gestured toward the front yard of the residence and moved in its direction. But he only got two steps before Ray cried out in sorrow and fell to his knees.

Rayneshia stared at her father, suddenly fearful now, because next to Sharon's death, there were only two others that could make him break down this way. Her and her mother. She was alive and well, and ... Rayneshia felt her heart constrict with agonizing fear.

"Daddy, what's wrong?" she asked. When her father looked up into her eyes, that was when Rayneshia knew. The truth shone in the weariness of his sad eyes.

Qay was there to catch her when Rayneshia's knees buckled beneath her.

Ten minutes later, it was confirmed that Latrice Williams was dead, and Tami had killed Remmy. A reliable source broke down what had taken place back at the hospital. Von had struck again and so had Tami, whose safety was now Cody's ultimate concern.

After phoning his mother and speaking with her, Cody was convinced that his mother was indeed okay. She was with Daisy at the hospital on Bebop's behalf.

"Mama Tee is the truth," said Avery, as they all huddled upon the front lawn. Money Mel was working his phone from the porch steps, trying to see if he could get a lead on Von's position.

Detective Ray Williams was now considered armed and dangerous, as he got back in his car and roared away. He was a man scorned. Ray was liable to self-destruct if he wasn't careful.

"I say we go over to Tallahassee anyway and see what we can do from there," suggested Teddy.

"You think she went back to her turf now?" asked Cody.

"Nah," said Avery. "Like Daisy said earlier, Von is too unpredictable. We thought the same thang earlier, and the whole time, she was still here."

"And she's still here," said Po'Boy.

"What about the thang wit' her son?" said Avery.

Teddy looked at him curiously. "What son? What a crazy bitch like her doing wit' a fuckin' kid?"

"She 'bout to learn the hard way," Po'Boy replied, as he broke off to go speak with Felicia.

There was a moment of silence between the younger brothas, as the situation they were now faced with was building up to a bursting effect.

Money Mel approached them, and the look on his face was sterner than before the phone call.

"Why you lookin' like that, brah?" Avery asked.

"'Cause shit always happenin' when you least expect it to," said Money Mel.

"What happened now?"

"Von's son was taken as planned," he replied. "Then he was taken back by somebody else just now." Money Mel shook his head and sighed miserably.

***

Nineteen minutes ago, little Shyleek Branch was sitting before the large TV screen in the family room of the big condominium apartment, watching cartoons. His legal guardians were Yarissa and TJ Branch, one a professional real estate agent and the other a fifth grade teacher. TJ was gone already while Yarissa was preparing to enjoy her day away from the office with her baby boy. She had great plans for them, and even Shy seemed to be very much aware of the day's events.

With a mutual agreement, the Branches adopted Shy from Von with the exception that Von provided for him and visited him monthly. Shy knew Von was his mother, and that was okay with the Branches. The contentment came with Yarissa being more hands on with the child and sharing with him what only a real true mother should share with her child.

After Von learned that the Branches couldn't bear a child, she thought they were the perfect pair. It was her who reached out to Yarissa, and a deal was made. Both parents knew of Von's real true caliber, and it did not bother them much. Von made it her business to keep the existence of her son under wraps, and for more than two years now, she'd been honoring that.

But that was until Yarissa looked up from her cup of coffee at the huge chef island and found two armed goons standing in the kitchen doorway.

The cat was out the bag.

Her greatest fear.

And that was when Moo Moo upped his silenced pistol and pumped two slugs into her chest.

"Take some of his toys and shit that'll keep 'em calm for after we snatch him," said Moo Moo to his female comrade with the semi-automatic chrome pistol. She nodded and disappeared from sight.

Removing himself from the kitchen, Moo Moo reentered the large family room where Naomie was sitting next to the child on the floor, watching TV. She looked up at him in quiet understanding, and Moo Moo nodded reassuringly. It was she who'd be handling Shy on a more personal level. This was her way of warming up to him while engaging him with conversation regarding the cartoons he was watching.

"Done." Fejah appeared just behind Moo Moo with the kid's carry bag containing essentials and goodies.

Moo Moo glanced down at her gloved hands and knew how instinctively precautious she was. It was one of the qualities he respected about her. Fejah was older but serious about her position and was fearless as ever.

"Let's get it done," said Moo Moo.

And that was when Naomie produced the orange cloth that she covered Shy's face with. The boy put up a weak effort to fight her off, but unconsciousness took over him in a hurry. Then, Naomie disposed of the unconscious child into the large duffel bag she'd brought along. This way, when they left the building, no one could actually say that they saw the kid in their possession.

Fejah stuffed the carry bag into the duffel with the child, and they then took their leave.

Instead of taking the elevator down, the three of them took the stairs to the ground floor. No sooner than they entered the lobby did the elevator doors open, and a Black couple emerged.

With Moo Moo being the leader and the more ruthless one of the crew, he led the way toward the exit behind the couple before them. Naomi, who had the duffel strapped over her shoulder, walked with precision as she followed the path led by her superior.

Once outside in the morning sunshine, a '22 Volkswagen ID4 Pro pulled up to the curb outside the big condominium structure. Behind the wheel was Kato, and lying across the lap of his Kapital jeans was a strap.

"Everythang Kosher?" Kato asked after they all got in.

"You already know," answered Fejah.

"Where to now?"

"Where else, nigga? The only place we need to be right now is in Sherwood," said Moo Moo. Then, he blazed up a blunt he was smoking earlier.

The Volkswagen nosed its way toward the exit route of Beach Boulevard behind another vehicle. The first car stopped to wait its turn to pull out. Moo Moo passed Kato the blunt just as two bodies suddenly appeared on either side of the Volkswagen.

"Watch out!" screamed Naomie in alarm.

Instantly, Moo Moo lifted up his weapon, and a hail of bullets tore through the door into his body. On the other side, Kato and Fejah hollered with deathly cries as the second gunman filled their bodies with hot lead.

When the gunshots fell silent, the rear passenger door opened, and the big duffel bag was removed from the ruins and then placed into the lead car.

"On the money," said Sevin, who was behind the wheel of the Crown Vic. In the front passenger seat sat Shawn Henry, the big brother of BJ and one of Jacksonville's respected Kutthroat gang affiliates.

"You good, Magnolia?" asked Shawn, glancing back to look at K-Gutter in the backseat.

"Just anotha day in the trenches," K-Gutter rescinded as he switched magazines on his gun with a fresh one.

Meanwhile, the Crown Vic turned onto Beach Boulevard and took the Matthews Bridge to get to where their planned destination was. By the time they made it to MLK Boulevard and onward to Golfair Boulevard, the incident back at the condominiums was an afterthought.

Northside territory wasn't that far away, and before they knew it, the Crown Vic was cruising down Helena Street and parked behind a fenced in residence. Before the car parked itself, the back door of the house opened, and there stood Sasha in her booty shorts and a 9mm.

"Where the hell he at?" she asked.

"In here." K-Gutter lifted up the duffel bag he had carried out of the car.

Sasha looked at him like he'd lost his damn mind. "I know damn well you niggas ain't got that child in a fuckin' duffel bag," she snapped.

Shawn stepped past her to enter the house, and Sasha shot him a look so mean. Then, she demanded that the child be released from the bag, so she could see him with her own eyes.

"He still alive," said K-Gutter, who was Sasha's little brother and her pride and joy. This was the only nigga she had ever killed for next to Shawn, who was her man and K-Gutter's superior.

The second her brother entered the house after Shawn, he opened the bag to reveal the child. He was still unconscious but looked greatly disturbed. Sasha reached down and lifted the child up into her arms and carried him away from them.

"You talked to your brotha yet?" asked Sasha.

Shawn said, "I'm 'bout to hit him up now. I wanted to make sure we got away safely before I contacted him because we really need to have a serious talk 'bout what happened back at the…"

"What happened?"

Kato entered the living room from the kitchen carrying a can of Sunkist orange soda. "What happened is that some other muthafuckas had beat us to the punch, and we had to get busy."

"What? Who?"

"Moo Moo and 'em," said Shawn.

When he said the name, Sasha had to take a seat to gather her nerves. Shyleek was lying down on the same sofa to her left. Sasha couldn't believe what she had just heard.

It was Kato who had spotted Moo Moo and his female enforcers first. There was something about the way they moved that alerted him that something was up. He automatically knew that whatever it was that they were up to, it had to have something to do with the child. That was when Shawn decided to wait them out to see what happened next.

It was no secret who Moo Moo was and what he did in the streets. He was a killer, and his two companions were his loyal sidekicks. They answered under Bald Head, who was a local crime boss and Sasha's grandfather. And Moo Moo used to be her man way back when she was just earning her reputation, seven years before Shawn came along and made her his woman.

The death of Moo Moo and his crew would bring a lot of heat in the streets. And if Bald Head had any say in this, there would be a lot to worry about.

"You couldn't even avoid it, huh?" said Sasha, and her brother and Shawn looked at her meaningfully.

"It was either that or let them take the boy," Kato answered humbly.

"You know there's gonna be drama behind this?"

Shawn shrugged and said, "I live for drama, and I can demolish it too."

And that was what she was afraid of. Sasha was pregnant with her own child. And the last thing she needed was a street war right now.

Chapter 16

"Who is this nigga, Rikah?" Twan asked once they had settled down at a reserved table in Passion's Diner and Cafe, which was one of the establishments that Rikah owned.

They had left the dungeon for the diner where Rikah had a scheduled meeting with one of her business associates. Sitting at a nearby table was Rod, Souljah, and Dez with their heads forward, evidently conducting a serious conversation.

Outside the building, Jazz and Savage and the rest of the watchout team were in position. It had been confirmed that the STB crew was out there raising hell and calling themselves targeting Rikah and what all she'd built. But little did Remmy know that she had two of her own men inside his crew. They were reliable enough to put a stop to whatever it was they had going on without Rikah having to say too much.

But it still wasn't safe enough to let her guard down — not ever would it be safe to do such. That was why Rikah kept a team of killas at her beck and call.

"His name is Kordae Oliver. He's from Stockbridge, Georgia but lives in Atlanta working as a professional celebrity photographer and a sensational blogger. He and Alisha had tied the knot three years ago. The man is under the impression that his wife is medical personnel in the Air Force," said Rikah before raising her glass to taste her wine.

"And what about the little boy?"

"His name is Khalani."

Twan paused at the eloquence of the name.

"That's your middle name, I know. Khalani is almost three years old this coming November. To her husband, she is Temica Davis before they married, to who we both know as Alisha. But…"

Twan interrupted. "I can't believe my sista was doing all this shit without my knowing. Even having a baby and not tellin' me shit!" He frowned.

"Khalani isn't biologically hers, Twan. His real mama had complications during birth, and she never made it out."

"She died having him?" Twan was shocked by this matter. "What type of complications?" he asked.

"Heavy bleeding and some other shit."

"And the boy?"

"He's perfect in all aspects," said Rikah. "He's smart, gifted, and cute as ever."

For a long moment, Twan didn't say anything, as he took all this in. "How do you know so much about the shit and not me?"

"Another reason why I keep tellin' you that you should get out more often than you do. Anyway, I ran into her one day about a year ago in ATL. She was wit' her husband on this day. They were at the same gas station together when I pulled up." Rikah reached for her glass again.

"I bet that shocked the shit outta her."

"Shocked is an understatement, Twan. She was terrified."

"Did she tell you the truth then?"

She shook her head no. "That came later when she felt the need to face me," said Rikah.

Again, Twan didn't respond for a long time. Then, his phone sounded off. It was on the table beside him, and he reached to retrieve it. When he saw who it was, Twan's adrenaline surged like a head rush.

"I feel like you've double crossed me, old friend."

"Huh? What?" Twan stiffened. The person he was talking to was Chuck Murphy, the nephew of Bald Head West and the third-in-command next to his father, who was currently dying from cancer. Chuck was Twan's Jacksonville resource and a damn good business associate. But it was the tone in which Chuck just used to express himself that made Twan believe that the mission didn't go too well.

"You call me to help you with a problem, but you failed to inform me that you've employed someone else to handle the mission," said Chuck.

"Someone else? Hell naw!"

"Apparently, I wasn't the only one you told about this situation," said Chuck.

"You was the only one I told."

"Then why is my goddaughter and her crew dead, and the little rabbit was taken from them in the process, Antwan?" When those words left Chuck's mouth, Twan felt a sickness in his stomach.

"I don't know nothin' about that, Chuck, but I intend on finding out."

"So, you didn't mention this to no one?"

"Not a soul."

"Then you're not the only one who wants that rabbit, old friend. I respect you, Antwan, and I believe you wouldn't lie to me. Lies right now isn't the best move when I've lost loved ones. I'm sure you'll find out who's behind this and report back to me."

"Most definitely," Twan assured him.

"And I'll keep you posted as well."

"Thank you, Chuck."

"Don't disappoint me, Antwan," he replied. The line went dead.

When Twan looked up into Rikah's eyes, he read the question that they held.

"When you said you'd take care of it, I took you on your word, Antwan. I don't wanna hear no excuses. Just do your part," said Rikah.

All Twan could do was nod his head and get up and leave the diner.

At this time, Dez ceased all conversation and rose up to her feet to follow him outside. The look on his face was way too serious to ignore. Twan looked like he wanted to kill somebody.

The moment he stepped outside, Souljah was there to intercept the damage that was about to come when a body suddenly bumped into Twan's. The guy didn't expect someone to come charging out the door at the same time he was charging in, but Twan was moving like a freight train and didn't budge nor swerve when the door opened at just the right time. Souljah saved the guy from falling over, not knowing that he was the powerful business associate that Rikah was meeting with in the diner.

"What's the deal?" asked Dez after catching up with Twan's long strides.

"The mission was compromised just now."

"The kid?" she asked.

He glanced at her and stopped. "My people had done their part, but somebody else had the same intentions. I gotta find out who that somebody is," said Twan.

"So, we're going to Duval then?" Rod spoke up.

"That's what it looks like, brah." Twan looked at him and said, "We gotta get that boy back."

"I know," Dez sighed.

Rod said, "It's the only way we can stop Von."

No sooner than the words left his mouth did the atmosphere around them explode in gunfire. Automatic rounds rang out as three gunmen suddenly appeared from around the corner of the diner's building. Twan and the others reached for their weapons while ducking for cover, trying not to get hit. But the inevitable was too great. The enemy had the element of surprise, catching them off guard.

Three against a total of seven of them were odds that were determined to change the game.

It was the STB gang that had come to wreak havoc.

Three the hard way.

Total chaos.

***

The Cadillac Escalade was parked behind a yellow and green bungalow on Davis Street, over in the Hillside area.

The house belonged to Michelle Jackson, who was originally from out in Chattahoochee. She was Turk's baby mama, Ciera's cousin — the very same chick who he had had a short fling with prior to messing with Ciera. But the love and respect was still there, which was why Michelle didn't hesitate to welcome him and his crew inside.

That was where Von had been lying low since the incident back at the hospital. She figured that by now, she was a wanted woman. After all, Von expected this way before deciding to take the mission.

The detective's murder got the reaction she wanted from Ray, but the death of his wife was the topping on the cake. There was no doubt in her mind that Ray would employ enforcement from every authorized badge in the force to gun for her. But that could only happen if he still had an alliance in the department. Because, after all, Ray seemed to be the root of the problem, which was why all those he was close to were dying.

Von had spent some quality time in the bathroom with Yellow, engaged in a heart-to-heart conversation while he tended to her flesh wound. It was a painful task, but Von fought through it. It was also during that time that Von got to know Yellow on a much deeper level. He cleaned her wound, bandaged it up, and kissed the top of her head gently.

Afterwards, Turk beckoned them into the living room where he shared some important things with them regarding their situation.

"Lil Herb and Pusha are dead," said Turk, placing the cell phone on the table in front of him.

"How?" Yellow asked.

"This is gon' fuck you up, but I'm being told that Dutch was the one that did it."

"No."

Turk nodded and shrugged. "I was just on the phone wit' Suge, and he said he saw Dutch, Lil Herb, and Pusha get in the same car earlier. Dutch got in the back by himself. Both of them were shot in the back of the head. Dutch was later seen at the bus terminal around the corner from the murder scene like nothing even happened. So, you tell me if that's suspicious or not," he said.

"Why would he kill his own brothas?" Yellow asked.

"Because," said Von, "he's one of Rikah's people. Why else would he risk that move?"

"So, Dutch's an infiltrator?" said Yellow, shocked.

No one answered.

The next sound that came was Von's gun exploding as she shot Turk in the face. Yellow jumped to his feet at once and headed straight down the hall where Michelle was occupying her bedroom.

Two shots rang out a second later, and Von knew her young gunner was reacting off of instinct. He didn't give Michelle time to react and possibly ring the alarm.

"We don't move just yet," said Von. "We wait it out just in case somebody heard the gunshots and wonderin' where they came from. We remain humble until the time permits us to move."

"Turk and Dutch were closer to one another than the rest of the crew," said Yellow.

Von nodded. "You're the only one I trust right now, boo. And you know how I am wit' trusting people, Yellow." She held his gaze firmly.

"You can trust me, Vee. I won't let you down."

"Put that on somethin'?"

Yellow looked her dead in the eyes. "That's on my baby girl, Eboni," he said.

At the mention of his five-year-old sister, Von knew he was firm in his vow to her. Yellow would die for his little sister. He had killed her own father a little over a year ago for hurting her feelings. So, when it came down to Eboni, her big brother didn't play any games. Von nodded and saluted him respectively.

"So, we go after Dutch now?" asked Yellow. He and Dutch were as tight as brothas go, but at the end of the day, Dutch was disloyal, and disloyalty warranted death.

Without saying a word, Von reached for Turk's phone and checked his call log and recent text messages. He had received four texts from Dutch, implicating them in being tied with Rikah and discussing how they should go about executing the plan of attack against the team.

"He coulda killed both of us," whispered Von.

"What?"

Von growled viciously and closed her eyes, and Yellow took the phone away from her. He scanned the messages and cursed under his breath.

The truth was right before his eyes. At any time, Turk could have taken him out. And he could have gotten away with it too. Yellow was furious after seeing that he was so close to dying and didn't even know.

Von's own phone sounded off with its significant ringtone, indicating that it was TJ Branch calling. When she saw the number pop up on the screen, Von felt a jolt of dismay move her.

She answered hesitantly. "Hello."

"You lied to us," came a man's sorrowful voice. "You promised!"

Von shifted uneasily in her seat. "What happened, TJ?" she replied as a storm began to rage inside of her.

"They killed my wife and took our son!" Just those words alone brought so much fear in Von's heart that it stole her breath away. TJ Branch was a man that didn't scare easily, and right about now, he was as scared as a frightened child.

"TJ, I need for you to calm down for a second. I need you to send me the video footage from the door cam we had installed. Can you do that for me, TJ?" Von believed that if anybody knew about Shyleek, it would be Daisy or his real father, Mullet. But Mullet was dead because Von killed him with her own two hands when she was four months pregnant. So, that left Daisy, and the current beef between the two of them was more than likely her doing to get what she wanted.

Von's life was the price.

It was over.

There was no doubt in Von's mind that she would give her life to save her son's. Her mother and Reyzyne were collateral damage to reach this level of the game to really get the upper hand.

"I'll send it," said TJ miserably. "I'm at the station right now though."

"You told them…" Von blurted out.

"No, no," said TJ. "I never mentioned you or the door cam. But they're at the house right now, and it won't be long before they discover it."

"Don't let them find it, TJ!"

"Just find Shy and bring him home safely. Lemme do the rest," cried TJ Branch. The man was crazy about his wife and losing her today might just become his downfall.

Von spoke with the man another minute to reassure him that she would see that Shy made it back. She would do everything in her power to save her son from further harm.

If Daisy had him indeed, Von didn't believe that she would kill him. Daisy didn't kill kids. They had had a falling out about that once before when they were on a murder mission.

"It's over wit', ain't it?" Yellow said, snatching her out of her reverie.

Slowly, Von turned her gaze on her young bull, and she would have sworn she saw tears brimming in his eyes. "I love you, Yellow. I love my life too. But I love my son more than all that."

"So, you gon' do it? You gon' make that sacrifice?"

"Don't got no choice," she said evenly.

That was when a lone tear fell from Yellow's eye, and he turned away from her. Then, he exited the room for somewhere up the hallway out of sight.

A few tears fell from Von's eyes, and she hastily swiped them away. She growled deeply in her chest, as the pain constricted her will to stay calm.

"Fuck this shit!" said Yellow.

Von looked up and saw him moving toward her. She braced herself, and Yellow pushed her back against the sofa chair. When his lips met hers, she was lost for a moment. Then, her panties and shorts were snatched down to her ankles, legs thrown over his shoulders, and then Yellow drove nothing but hard dick into her in one fluid motion.

"Yellow!" she gasped.

"Tell me you love me again." Yellow long stroked her pussy with his eighteen-year-old manhood. He was in beast mode, and Von's pussy was under assault.

She didn't give him what he wanted.

He pounded harder.

"Tell me!" Yellow roared.

No reply.

Yellow went ballistic then. "You gon' do what the fuck I say, or I'ma break your shit," he told her.

"Break it then," was all Von said.

And break her down he tried, right there in the room with a dead body.

Shit was crazy.

Chapter 17

Tami leaned forward and put her head in her hands and let out a troubled breath. She was fighting the pain and the outrage that threatened to explode from her soul. She felt like her heart was about to burst.

Bebop had just been released from surgery ten minutes ago. That bullet that struck him in his lower back destroyed the vertebrae near the tailbone, rendering him paralyzed from the waist down. The bullet had done some serious damage with just only a nick of the lower spinal region. It was said that Bebop would never walk again.

And it hurt Tami to her soul to hear that coming from a certified surgeon who had been doing this type of work for more than forty years.

Tami refused to leave Bebop's side. She knew once he awakened, Bebop would need someone he loved and trusted to be there with him because once reality hit him, it could destroy him further. Many others in similar situations had faced their realities and became victims to suicide. There was no telling what his twelve-year-old brain would resort to when the same thing happened to ten-year-old Brittany Lewin up in Boston, and she swallowed poison on purpose to kill herself.

Depression was a serious matter.

It was dangerous.

And children were not exempt to its ugliness.

Tami wanted so badly to find his real mother, Evette, and rip her fucking heart out with her bare hands. She would be doing the world a favor anyway. Evette was a serious dope addict, and she had no love for her own child. If it wasn't for Tami and her sistas and their children, Bebop's life would be miserable to the highest degree. They brought light into his life and color into his world. Bebop was theirs just as much as he was his no-good mother's.

But Evette was in the county jail serving time right now for a list of crimes. She never did have her priorities right, always focused on her next fix.

As for Bebop's father, no one knew, and nobody was willing to take claim.

Despite his young, hard life, Bebop was smarter than the average twelve-year-old. He was thorough by street trade, and he was loved by many. Young Bebop had been there for the hood he was raised in like none other. Without him, a lot of lives would have been lost if he hadn't earned the trust of the right people.

Now, Bebop was down and out, and Tami wondered who was going to be there for him as he was them.

Who would step up to the plate?

Tami straightened herself up and rose up to her feet to stand at Bebop's bedside.

"I'll always be by your side, baby," she whispered to him and rubbed the back of his head softly. Bebop was lying on his stomach to stay off his back. More tests were scheduled to be examined by a second opinionated doctor.

The door opened, making Tami look in its direction, and she didn't expect to see Twan step inside. He had blood all on his clothes, and that made her turn fully around toward him.

"It's not mine," said Twan, closing the door behind him.

"Then whose is it, Twan?" she asked.

"Someone I was very fond of."

"Who?"

"Jazmyne Hayes but we call her Jazz."

"What happened to her?"

"She died just now," said Twan.

Tami dropped her head as if it hurt her to see the pain in his eyes.

He told her about the gun battle outside Rikah's restaurant an hour ago. Malik, Jazz, and Souljah were killed, while two of the shooters died in the process. The third shooter ran away with Rod and Dez chasing after him, trying to blow his head off.

"Did they get 'em?" Tami asked.

"That's being determined now because we've yet to hear back from him or her."

"You don't think they're hurt or anythang, do you?" Bebop moaned in his sleep, and Tami reached down to rub the back of his head again.

"I don't know what to think or believe right now, Tami," he said in exasperation. He moved closer to Bebop's bedside and stared down upon him quietly. Then, he shook his head sadly and asked, "Does his big brothas know what the doctor's saying about his condition?"

"Not yet. No," muttered Tami.

"Another thang to worry about."

Tami said, "It's gonna kill them to see him like that now, Cody especially because they were the closest." She paused for a long moment. "I don't know when the last time it's been this bad, Twan."

"I know when."

"What happened?"

He continued. "Hooliganz Crime Gang. It was the biggest street takeover in Quincy history. Remember the club massacre in St. Hebron about eight years ago? And some years before then, that big war between the Hooliganz and your old homeboy, Lyonell? About fifty people died in one day." Twan was bringing her mind back to the HCG and the ruthlessness that they brought to their small town in the form of a gang of youngstas who killed without mercy and had the drug game in a chokehold. It started off with five young neighborhood friends — four boys and a girl — and through them came the biggest, deadliest small-town gang that Qunicy had ever bred. In about a seven-year stretch, Hooliganz Crime Gang had developed larger than ever; many had been killed in a series of major bloodshed, leaving just a handful left. But those were rarely seen or heard from. Yet they were still spoke of with street reverence, respect, or fear.

"It's been that long, Twan?" asked Tami.

"Since Skinny got killed."

"Your half brotha."

He nodded. That was two siblings he'd lost, and Twan was still affected by Skinny's murder.

Again, the door opened, and this time, Daisy entered the room. She was followed by Rikah and two of her certified shooters, Brazy and Tuk.

This was the first time Tami and Rikah had seen one another in over a year. When they came face to face at that moment, it was as though the two couldn't wait to see each other. Rikah and Tami hugged one another for a very long time.

"Any word yet on Dez?" Twan asked Daisy. It was not long ago, after meeting Daisy there at the hospital, that he learned about BJ's hand in securing the boy through his people.

"Still no answer yet, Twan, but she's wit' Rod, and you know he ain't gon' let nothin' happen to her if he got somethin' to do wit' it."

"I sure hope so," said Rikah. "But I like Rod to keep her in check."

"But for how long though? How long before she murders him next for pushin' her? At this level, Dez is the most dangerous to anybody rather than to herself," said Twan, who believed that he knew Dez enough to determine how and where her rattled brain would take her. "My greatest concern is gettin' the lil' boy back, so we can do what we need to do," he added.

"About that too, Twan," said Daisy. "What are your intentions for him after Von gives us what we want?"

"You really think Von gonna do it?"

"Wit' out a doubt," Daisy said.

Twan said, "I don't kill children, Daisy, if that's what you're gettin' at."

"That's exactly what I'm gettin' at."

"He'll be all yours to do wit' him whatever you feel is needed, cuz," Rikah interjected.

"Where's BJ anyway?" asked Daisy. "I thought he was wit' you, Rikah?"

"I was about to ask you the same thang, cuz. I thought he had come back wit' you."

Dread filled Daisy's heart instantly, as she moved toward the door. She snatched the door open, and there stood BJ before her, a confused expression written on his face, as he entered the room.

"Where you been, BJ?" Daisy willed her heart to slow its thriving pace. "You had me worried."

"Do y'all know Von's old boy is in the room two doors down from here?" said BJ.

Before anyone could answer, the door exploded open, as no less than ten armed Gangsta Disciples entered with grim faces. The only one fast enough to draw their weapon was Twan, and three guns were in turn aimed at his noggin.

"Make your move, my G," said the shorter GD member standing between the three shooters aiming their weapons at Twan.

"What do you want, AP?" Twan didn't back down.

"We only came here for one thang," said AP, obviously the leader of the pack. "Where is Von?"

To Be Continued…

Fresh Off Da Porch Part 3:
Slippaz Don't Count
By: Ira L. Bunion
-Ira B.-

Lock Down Publications and Ca$h Presents
Assisted Publishing Packages

Due to an increase in the price of services we have increased our prices. The prices below reflect the price increase as of 11/1/24.

BASIC PACKAGE $699 Editing Cover Design Formatting	UPGRADED PACKAGE $1000 Typing Editing Cover Design Formatting Upload eBooks to Amazon Upload Paperback to Amazon
ADVANCE PACKAGE $1,400 Typing Editing (line editing/content) Cover Design Formatting Copyright Registration Proofreading Upload eBooks to Amazon Upload Paperback to Amazon	LDP SUPREME PACKAGE $1,700 Typing Editing (line editing/content) Cover Design Formatting Copyright Registration Proofreading Set up Amazon Account Upload eBooks to Amazon Upload Paperback to Amazon Advertise on LDP's Amazon and Facebook Page

***
Other services available upon request.
Additional charges may apply

Lock Down Publications
P.O. Box 944
Stockbridge, GA 30281-9998
Phone: 470 303-9761
Email: lockdownpublications@gmail.com

Submission Guideline

Submit the first three chapters of your completed manuscript to ldpsubmissions@gmail.com. In the subject line add **Your Book's Title**. The manuscript must be in a Word Doc file and sent as an attachment. Document should be in Times New Roman, double spaced, and in size 12 font. Also, provide your synopsis and full contact information. If sending multiple submissions, they must each be in a separate email.

Have a story but no way to send it electronically? You can still submit to LDP/Ca$h Presents. Send in the first three chapters, written or typed, of your completed manuscript to:

LDP: Submissions Dept
P.O. Box 944
Stockbridge, GA 30281-9998

DO NOT send original manuscript. Must be a duplicate.
Provide your synopsis and a cover letter containing your full contact information.

Thanks for considering LDP and Ca$h Presents.

NEW RELEASES

BLOODLINE OF A SAVAGE 1-3
THESE VICIOUS STREETS 1-3
RELENTLESS GOON 1-3
BY PRINCE A. TAUHID

THE BUTTERFLY MAFIA 1-3
BY FUMIYA PAYNE

A THUG'S STREET PRINCESS 1&2
BY MEESHA

CITY OF SMOKE 3
BY MOLOTTI

GET IT IN SLUGS 1 &2
BY B. STALL

STANDING ON HER BUSINESS 1&2
BY DG SANTANA

STEPPERS 1,2&3
THE REAL BADDIES OF CHI-RAQ
BY KING RIO

THE LANE 1&2
BY KEN-KEN SPENCE

THUG OF SPADES 1&2
LOVE IN THE TRENCHES 2
CORNER BOYS
BY COREY ROBINSON

TIL DEATH 3
BY ARYANNA

FRESH OFF DA PORCH 2 | IRA B.

THE BIRTH OF A GANGSTER 4
BY DELMONT PLAYER

PRODUCT OF THE STREETS 1-3
BY DEMOND "MONEY" ANDERSON

NO TIME FOR ERROR
BY KEESE

MONEY HUNGRY DEMONS 1-2
BY TRANAY ADAMS

HUB CITY MENACE 1-3
BY J. WHITE

A THUGGISH PASSION 1&2
LAND OF DA HOOLIGANZ 1-4
KILLAZ ON STANDBY 1&2
BY IRA B.

FO'EVA ROLLIN 1&2
BY ASSA RAYMOND BAKER

THE LEVEL UP 1&3
BY LUXURY KING

Coming Soon from Lock Down Publications/Ca$h Presents

IF YOU CROSS ME ONCE 6
ANGEL V
By Anthony Fields

A THUGS STREET PRINCESS 3
By Meesha

CORNER BOYS 2
By Corey Robinson

THA TAKEOVER
By Keith Chandler

BETRAYAL OF A G 2
By Ray Vinci

SAVAGE FAMILY EMPIRE 1&2
SOULLESS GOON 1,2&3
THE DIRTY SIDE OF MONEY 1,2&3
By Prince

FOR MY ENEMY'S SAKE
AMBITIONS OF A SLIDER
FRESH OFF DA PORCH
By IRA B.

THE TRUCKLOAD 1-4
TIPPIN' THE SCALES 1-3
BAD BITCHES WIT GUNZ 3
PROBLEM SOLVED 2
By Christopher "Diesel" Hornezes

Available Now

RESTRAINING ORDER 1 & 2
By **CA$H & Coffee**

LOVE KNOWS NO BOUNDARIES 1-3
By **Coffee**

RAISED AS A GOON I, II, III & IV
BRED BY THE SLUMS I, II, III
BLAST FOR ME I & II
ROTTEN TO THE CORE I II III
A BRONX TALE I, II, III
DUFFLE BAG CARTEL I II III IV V VI
HEARTLESS GOON I II III IV V
A SAVAGE DOPEBOY I II
DRUG LORDS I II III
CUTTHROAT MAFIA I II
KING OF THE TRENCHES
By **Ghost**

LAY IT DOWN I & II
LAST OF A DYING BREED I II
BLOOD STAINS OF A SHOTTA I & II III
By **Jamaica**

LOYAL TO THE GAME I II III
LIFE OF SIN I, II III
By **TJ & Jelissa**

IF LOVING HIM IS WRONG...I & II
LOVE ME EVEN WHEN IT HURTS I II III
By **Jelissa**

PUSH IT TO THE LIMIT
By **Bre' Hayes**

BLOODY COMMAS I & II
SKI MASK CARTEL I, II & III
KING OF NEW YORK I II, III IV V
RISE TO POWER I II III
COKE KINGS I II III IV V
BORN HEARTLESS I II III IV
KING OF THE TRAP I II
By **T.J. Edwards**

WHEN THE STREETS CLAP BACK I & II III
THE HEART OF A SAVAGE I II III IV
MONEY MAFIA I II
LOYAL TO THE SOIL I II III
By **Jibril Williams**

A DISTINGUISHED THUG STOLE MY HEART I II & III
LOVE SHOULDN'T HURT I II III IV
RENEGADE BOYS 1-4
PAID IN KARMA 1-3
SAVAGE STORMS 1-3
AN UNFORESEEN LOVE 1-3
BABY, I'M WINTERTIME COLD 1-3
A THUG'S STREET PRINCESS 1&2
By **Meesha**

A GANGSTER'S CODE 1-3
A GANGSTER'S SYN 1-3
THE SAVAGE LIFE 1-3
CHAINED TO THE STREETS 1-3
BLOOD ON THE MONEY 1-3
A GANGSTA'S PAIN 1-3
BEAUTIFUL LIES AND UGLY TRUTHS
CHURCH IN THESE STREETS
By **J-Blunt**

CUM FOR ME 1-8
An LDP Erotica Collaboration

FRESH OFF DA PORCH 2 | IRA B.

BLOOD OF A BOSS 1-5
SHADOWS OF THE GAME
TRAP BASTARD
By **Askari**

THE STREETS BLEED MURDER 1-3
THE HEART OF A GANGSTA 1-3
By **Jerry Jackson**

WHEN A GOOD GIRL GOES BAD
By **Adrienne**

THE COST OF LOYALTY 1-3
By **Kweli**

BRIDE OF A HUSTLA 1-3
THE FETTI GIRLS 1-3
CORRUPTED BY A GANGSTA 1-4
BLINDED BY HIS LOVE
THE PRICE YOU PAY FOR LOVE 1-3
DOPE GIRL MAGIC 1-3
By **Destiny Skai**

A KINGPIN'S AMBITION
A KINGPIN'S AMBITION II
I MURDER FOR THE DOUGH
By **Ambitious**

TRUE SAVAGE 1-7
DOPE BOY MAGIC 1-3
MIDNIGHT CARTEL 1-3
CITY OF KINGZ 1&2
NIGHTMARE ON SILENT AVE
THE PLUG OF LIL MEXICO 1&2
CLASSIC CITY
By **Chris Green**

150

A GANGSTER'S REVENGE 1-4
THE BOSS MAN'S DAUGHTERS 1-5
A SAVAGE LOVE 1&2
BAE BELONGS TO ME 1&2
A HUSTLER'S DECEIT 1-3
WHAT BAD BITCHES DO 1-3
SOUL OF A MONSTER 1-3
KILL ZONE
A DOPE BOY'S QUEEN 1-3
TIL DEATH 1-3
IMMA DIE BOUT MINE 1-6
DYING FOR LIKES
By **Aryanna**

A DOPEBOY'S PRAYER
By **Eddie "Wolf" Lee**

THE KING CARTEL 1-3
By **Frank Gresham**

THESE NIGGAS AIN'T LOYAL 1-3
By **Nikki Tee**

GANGSTA SHYT 1-3
By **CATO**

THE ULTIMATE BETRAYAL
By **Phoenix**

BOSS'N UP 1-3
By **Royal Nicole**

I LOVE YOU TO DEATH
By **Destiny J**

I RIDE FOR MY HITTA
I STILL RIDE FOR MY HITTA
By **Misty Holt**

LOVE & CHASIN' PAPER
By **Qay Crockett**

TO DIE IN VAIN
SINS OF A HUSTLA
By **ASAD**

BROOKLYN HUSTLAZ
By **Boogsy Morina**

BROOKLYN ON LOCK 1 & 2
By **Sonovia**

GANGSTA CITY
By **Teddy Duke**

A DRUG KING AND HIS DIAMOND 1-3
A DOPEMAN'S RICHES
HER MAN, MINE'S TOO 1&2
CASH MONEY HO'S
THE WIFEY I USED TO BE 1&2
PRETTY GIRLS DO NASTY THINGS
By **Nicole Goosby**

LIPSTICK KILLAH 1-3
CRIME OF PASSION 1-3
FRIEND OR FOE 1-3
By **Mimi**

TRAPHOUSE KING 1-3
KINGPIN KILLAZ 1-3
STREET KINGS 1&2
PAID IN BLOOD 1&2
CARTEL KILLAZ 1-3
DOPE GODS 1&2
By **Hood Rich**

THE STREETS ARE CALLING
By **Duquie Wilson**

STEADY MOBBN' 1-3
THE STREETS STAINED MY SOUL 1-3
By **Marcellus Allen**

WHO SHOT YA 1-3
SON OF A DOPE FIEND 1-4
HEAVEN GOT A GHETTO 1&2
SKI MASK MONEY 1&2
By **Renta**

GORILLAZ IN THE BAY 1-4
TEARS OF A GANGSTA 1/&2
3X KRAZY 1&2
STRAIGHT BEAST MODE 1&2
By **DE'KARI**

TRIGGADALE 1-3
MURDA WAS THE CASE 1-3
By **Elijah R. Freeman**

SLAUGHTER GANG 1-3
RUTHLESS HEART 1-3
By **Willie Slaughter**

GOD BLESS THE TRAPPERS 1-3
THESE SCANDALOUS STREETS 1-3
FEAR MY GANGSTA 1-5
THESE STREETS DON'T LOVE NOBODY 1-2
BURY ME A G 1-5
A GANGSTA'S EMPIRE 1-4
THE DOPEMAN'S BODYGAURD 1&2
THE REALEST KILLAZ 1-3
THE LAST OF THE OGS 1-3
By **Tranay Adams**

MARRIED TO A BOSS 1-3
By **Destiny Skai & Chris Green**

KINGZ OF THE GAME 1-7
CRIME BOSS 1-4
By **Playa Ray**

FUK SHYT
By **Blakk Diamond**

DON'T F#CK WITH MY HEART 1&2
By **Linnea**

ADDICTED TO THE DRAMA 1-3
IN THE ARM OF HIS BOSS
By **Jamila**

LOYALTY AIN'T PROMISED 1&2
By **Keith Williams**

YAYO 1-4
A SHOOTER'S AMBITION 1&2
BRED IN THE GAME
By **S. Allen**

TRAP GOD 1-3
RICH $AVAGE 1-3
MONEY IN THE GRAVE 1-3
CARTEL MONEY 1&2
By **Martell Troublesome Bolden**

FOREVER GANGSTA 1&2
GLOCKS ON SATIN SHEETS 1&2
By **Adrian Dulan**

TOE TAGZ 1-4
LEVELS TO THIS SHYT 1&2
IT'S JUST ME AND YOU
By **Ah'Million**

KINGPIN DREAMS 1-3
RAN OFF ON DA PLUG
By **Paper Boi Rari**

THE STREETS MADE ME 1-3
By **Larry D. Wright**

CONFESSIONS OF A GANGSTA 1-4
CONFESSIONS OF A JACKBOY 1-3
CONFESSIONS OF A HITMAN
CONFESSIONS OF A DOPE BOY
By **Nicholas Lock**

I'M NOTHING WITHOUT HIS LOVE
SINS OF A THUG
TO THE THUG I LOVED BEFORE
A GANGSTA SAVED XMAS
IN A HUSTLER I TRUST
By **Monet Dragun**

QUIET MONEY 1-3
THUG LIFE 1-3
EXTENDED CLIP 1&2
A GANGSTA'S PARADISE
By **Trai'Quan**

CAUGHT UP IN THE LIFE 1-3
THE STREETS NEVER LET GO 1-3
By **Robert Baptiste**

NEW TO THE GAME 1-3
MONEY, MURDER & MEMORIES 1-3
By **Malik D. Rice**

CREAM 2-3
THE STREETS WILL TALK
By **Yolanda Moore**

THE STREETS WILL NEVER CLOSE 1-3
By **K'ajji**

LIFE OF A SAVAGE 1-4
A GANGSTA'S QUR'AN 1-4
MURDA SEASON 1-3
GANGLAND CARTEL 1-3
CHI'RAQ GANGSTAS 1-4
KILLERS ON ELM STREET 1-3
JACK BOYZ N DA BRONX 1-3
A DOPEBOY'S DREAM 1-3
JACK BOYS VS DOPE BOYS 1-3
COKE GIRLZ
COKE BOYS
SOSA GANG 1&2
BRONX SAVAGES
BODYMORE KINGPINS
BLOOD OF A GOON
By **Romell Tukes**

CONCRETE KILLA 1-3
VICIOUS LOYALTY 1-3
BLOODY MONEY BAGS
By **Kingpen**

THE ULTIMATE SACRIFICE 1-6
KHADIFI
IF YOU CROSS ME ONCE 1-3
ANGEL 1-4
IN THE BLINK OF AN EYE
By **Anthony Fields**

THE LIFE OF A HOOD STAR
By **Ca$h & Rashia Wilson**

NIGHTMARES OF A HUSTLA 1-3
BLOOD AND GAMES 1&2
By **King Dream**

GHOST MOB
By **Stilloan Robinson**

HARD AND RUTHLESS 1&2
MOB TOWN 251
THE BILLIONAIRE BENTLEYS 1-3
REAL G'S MOVE IN SILENCE
By **Von Diesel**

MOB TIES 1-7
SOUL OF A HUSTLER, HEART OF A KILLER 1-3
GORILLAZ IN THE TRENCHES
OOPS CRY TOO 1&2
THE DAUGHTER OF A CARTEL BOSS
By **SayNoMore**

BODYMORE MURDERLAND 1-3
THE BIRTH OF A GANGSTER 1-4
By **Delmont Player**

FOR THE LOVE OF A BOSS 1&2
By **C. D. Blue**

KILLA KOUNTY 1-5
TENDER
By **Khufu**

MOBBED UP 1-4
THE BRICK MAN 1-5
THE COCAINE PRINCESS 1-10
STEPPERS 1-3
SUPER GREMLIN 1-4
A GANGSTA'S SON
By **King Rio**

MONEY GAME 1&2
By **Smoove Dolla**

A GANGSTA'S KARMA 1-5
By **FLAME**

KING OF THE TRENCHES 1-3
By **GHOST & TRANAY ADAMS**

BAD BITCHES WIT GUNZ 1&2
PROBLEM SOLVED
By **"Christopher Diesel" Hornezes**

QUEEN OF THE ZOO 1&2
By **Black Migo**

GRIMEY WAYS 1-3
BETRAYAL OF A G
By **Ray Vinci**

XMAS WITH AN ATL SHOOTER
By **Ca$h & Destiny Skai**

KING KILLA 1&2
By **Vincent "Vitto" Holloway**

BETRAYAL OF A THUG 1&2
By **Fre$h**

COUNTDOWN OF A KILLA 1&2
SEX, MURDER AND GOD 1&2
GUNS DOWN, BOTTOMS UP 1&2
By Lo-Life

THE MURDER QUEENS 1-7
By **Michael Gallon**

FOR THE LOVE OF BLOOD 1-4
By **Jamel Mitchell**

FRESH OFF DA PORCH 2 | IRA B.

HOOD CONSIGLIERE 1&2
NO TIME FOR ERROR
By **Keese**

PROTÉGÉ OF A LEGEND 1,2&3
LOVE IN THE TRENCHES 1&2
By **Corey Robinson**

THE PLUG'S RUTHLESS DAUGHTER 1&2
By **Tony Daniels**

BORN IN THE GRAVE 1-3
CRIME PAYS
By **Self Made Tay**

MOAN IN MY MOUTH
By **XTASY**

TORN BETWEEN A GANGSTER AND A GENTLEMAN
By **J-BLUNT & Miss Kim**

LOYALTY IS EVERYTHING 1-3
CITY OF SMOKE 1-3
By **Molotti**

HERE TODAY GONE TOMORROW 1&2
By **Fly Rock**

WOMEN LIE MEN LIE 1-4
FIFTY SHADES OF SNOW 1-3
STACK BEFORE YOU SPLURGE
GIRLS FALL LIKE DOMINOES
NAÏVE TO THE STREETS
By **ROY MILLIGAN**

PILLOW PRINCESS
By **S. Hawkins**

THE BUTTERFLY MAFIA 1-3
SALUTE MY SAVAGERY 1&2
By **Fumiya Payne**

THE LANE 1&2
By Ken-Ken Spence

THE PUSSY TRAP 1-5
By **Nene Capri**

DIRTY DNA
By **Blaque**

SANCTIFIED AND HORNY
by **XTASY**

BOOKS BY LDP'S CEO, CA$H

TRUST IN NO MAN
TRUST IN NO MAN 2
TRUST IN NO MAN 3
BONDED BY BLOOD
SHORTY GOT A THUG
THUGS CRY
THUGS CRY 2
THUGS CRY 3
TRUST NO BITCH
TRUST NO BITCH 2
TRUST NO BITCH 3
TIL MY CASKET DROPS
RESTRAINING ORDER
RESTRAINING ORDER 2
IN LOVE WITH A CONVICT
LIFE OF A HOOD STAR
XMAS WITH AN ATL SHOOTER

www.ingramcontent.com/pod-product-compliance
Lightning Source LLC
Chambersburg PA
CBHW060420260626
47161CB00005B/1718